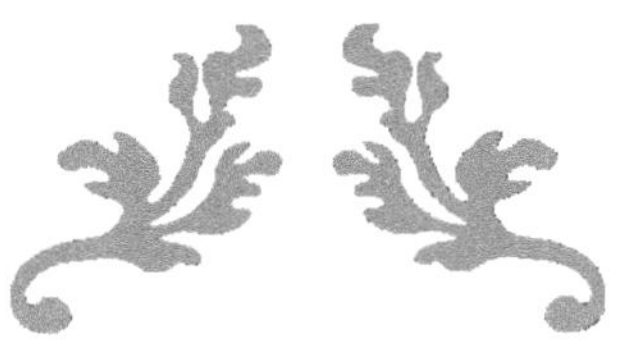

JESUS' MENTOR

ELIJAH

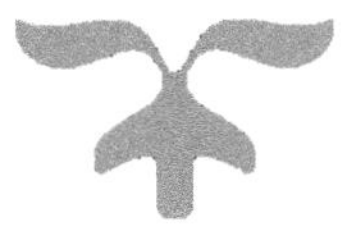

A HISTORICAL SCIENCE FICTION NOVAL

ROBERT RASCH

FOREWORD

ELIJAH: HISTORICAL BACKGROUND

- Mentor of Jesus and originator of the New Testament.
- Born February 12, 2015 in the Hercules Dome under the Polar Plateau, Antarctica.
- Miracle wonder worker from 852 BC to 860 BC.
- First prophet to raise someone from the dead.
- Known for his summer storms, hail, rain, thunder and dew.
- Fought to get rid of idolatry.
- Taken to the heavens in a whirlwind, in a lighted fire vehicle.
- Descended from the heavens and ascended back to the heavens.
- Author of the "Book of Elijah."

This story is based on information declassified from both the National Advisory Committee for Aeronautics *(NACA)* and the Vatican Archives. NACA was a U.S. federal agency founded on March 3, 1915 to undertake, promote and institutionalize aeronautical research. On October 1, 1958, the agency was dissolved, and its assets and personnel were transferred to the newly created National Aeronautics and Space Administration *(NASA)*. The Vatican Archives cannot confirm the Book of Elijah but does confirm that some of his works are in their possession.

This story is time released by the author for the benefit and preparation of the human race so they may gain an understanding and broader view of their historic ancestors and custodians who to this day oversee this sector and galaxy in space.

****

There are some lives that are like no others, rising beyond the norm at a perplexing and astonishing rate. The young boy Elijah grew and matured into a great motivator, thinker, and innovator with a profound effect on others. By believing in his very own *probability theory* and with great discipline, he paved a way that changed the fabric of man's destiny that is embraced up to this very day.

Elijah's teachings would resonate throughout the ages, greatly impacting religious factions. His mentor was his father, Aligious, who instilled in him virtues of humility and selflessness that can only be described as divinely inspired.

Aligious was "the architect of the Old Testament" while Elijah would become, unknowingly, the creator of the New Testament. Elijah's life would eventually reveal the hidden perspectives and in-betweens of Jesus' full existence from birth to His "Second Coming."

ELIJAH

"To live in harmony is to be truly living."

"Understanding relations is synonymous with distance."

"Worrying is just a poor way of praying."

"A gift is not a gift unless it is received."

A special thanks to my family and friends for sharing their research, as well as their advice.

The quotes and theories from this book have been taken from many different sources and are not intended to offend or sway any personal beliefs that are core to the reader.

TABLE OF CONTENTS

Foreword 1

Chapter One Childhood 5

Chapter Two The Meeting 10

Chapter Three Zobzball 12

Chapter Four Boyhood 16

Chapter Five The Moon 21

Chapter Six Historic Data Machine 27

Chapter Seven Eight-Year Ministry 30

Chapter Eight The Quietus 34

Chapter Nine Ministry Conclusion 37

Chapter Ten Cave Innovation 39

Chapter Eleven Articles of Faith 50

Chapter Twelve The Birth Choice 52

Chapter Thirteen Mentor 58

Chapter Fourteen Desert 67

Chapter Fifteen Three-Year Ministry 70

Chapter Sixteen The Passion 72

Chapter Seventeen Crucifixion 94

Chapter Eighteen The Resurrection 102

Chapter Nineteen The Second Coming 106

Chapter Twenty Integration 109

The Book Of Elijah 111

About The Author 113

Chapter One

Childhood

The City of Adelaide in the summer is typically bright and temperate which young Elijah did not mind. Waiting for his father to pick him up from school, he casually strolled from the Atrium Erudition School to their meeting place in between the pyramid structures in anticipation of his father's arrival.

Watching the people hurried past him in all directions, it seemed as if they were being herded like sheep between the structures. Elijah studied the precise angles of the pyramids' architecture, the uniquely chiseled stonework and the flowing waters of the fountain and understood why his father would want to meet here.

As he looked ahead, he saw his father waiting for him. Tall and broad with locks of silvery long hair, Aligious has a commanding presence but in a non-intimidating way. In his son's eyes, his father was great in so many ways. Aligious was in charge of overseeing Earth's occupants and was well respected amongst the people.

Elijah quickened his stride and as eye contact was made, a great excitement consumed him. He shook his father's hand in the classic Mazone style, (please describe in a couple of words the Mazone style), which is the customary father and son handshake.

"I have a very important meeting I need to attend with the Elders in the Aitho Circle Towers," Aligious said.

Elijah sighed and was initially disappointed. He then realized the importance of the meeting to his father and agreed to join Aligious. He understood he had to sacrifice the planned sport and game time with him.

They stepped inside a Meta Mechin Gate machine which is unusual because Elijah knew his father loved to travel the conventional way, on foot. "What is the meeting about?" asked Elijah, unable to control his curiosity any longer.

Aligious exhaled and looked up at the machine, not responding to Elijah's question. He spoke aloud commands while staring into the machine, dictating the coordinates of their destination into the location receptor.

He then looked down at Elijah and said, "One moment, son, first let us go through." A loud sound emanated as if water was being crystallized. The noise continued to grow louder and louder until it suddenly softened to a tolerable hum. Seconds later, they arrived at the Aitho Circle Towers and exited the Meta Mechin Gate machine.

Aligious turned to Elijah and said, "We will stay in the lobby area while I wait for the eleven Elders to arrive. When they arrive, I have to go to the Conference Hall, and you have to stay in the lobby because minors are not allowed entry into the hall."

"To answer your question earlier, the Council of Elders and I are responsible for influencing what happens on Earth, mainly on the surface," Aligious continued. "It may seem confusing to you now, son, but when you turn twenty-one years of age, you will be able to receive the Synoptic Learn Ids and have an amazing amount of data and knowledge at your disposal. For now, certain information is restricted from the circle of youths."

Aligious laughed heartily and winked at Elijah, "But, I will tell you an abbreviated version about the Elders and where they originated from while we are waiting."

Elijah's eyes brightened with great interest and he went closer to his father. It was the conversation that would one day inspire Elijah to spawn creative ideas that will have a major influence in Earth's development.

"The Arcturians have the most advanced and eloquent civilization in our galaxy," began Aligious. They have gifted and guided our collective galactic staff to agreements of peace and continuity amongst the Union of Worlds. In addition, they also protect the Earth by preventing any one Faction from dominating the geographic regions of the globe, thereby establishing a healthy balance."

Elijah listened attentively while Aligious further explained, "The places of origin amongst the factions led us to an understanding that our native planets, size, location and atmospheric conditions determine the foundation of development. This historical observation has produced proof that races of different worlds can be productive in a spiritual way, fulfilling a harmonious result while moving forward. The Elders feel responsible for these forward improvements that is predestined for almost all intellectual entities/species."

Aligious looked away and thought of his upcoming meeting. It is about to start, but then stared at Elijah and said, "Come with me, son. I will take you to the Athenaeum. It is a wondrous building that will intrigue you architecturally, but also houses some of the best recorded historical visuals that will better explain the important parts of our conversation."

Elijah realized his father's sacrifice of the moment, to share in his curiosity. They entered the Athenaeum with high trilateral pyramid vaulted ceilings and the "Vertex Globe" at its highest point.

Aligious turned on the Vertex Globe and it immediately started producing swirls of plasma gas waves. An energized light suddenly became apparent at the apex of the pyramid. He commanded the module with his voice and an entire three-dimensional layout of the galaxy appeared; stars, planets, satellites, space stations, asteroids, and clusters of orbits and wormholes connected together.

Elijah opened his mouth in astonishment and asked, "All the solar systems of the sector seems to tie together in perfect harmony. How does everything become so organized from chaos?"

Aligious explained, "Eli, everything created in and of the Universe has an absolute supreme imprint of selected intelligence. The same way the 3D Vertex simulation can let you see the circuitry of neurons or arteries within your body, it can let you see the vascular weaving of wormholes."

Elijah was intrigued and in awe, walking and spinning through the middle of the holographic galaxy. He waved his hand through the mapped star system, with no effect on it, and enjoyed the stunning moving display.

"Oh, I love this," Elijah exclaimed, forgetting the missed sport and game time. "Are these wormholes in any way the invisible connective bio frequencies?"

"No and yes," Aligious answered. "They are mainly a means of travel between two points of time and location, connecting and linking all that you see here in the galaxy. I'll explain."

Elijah quickly stopped moving through the holographic display and paid attention to his father.

"The wormholes are the corridors that take someone or something from point A to B," began Aligious. "Basically, to start the transport process, let's say, to and from our planet to Earth, a phase transition takes place. Waves of plasma cause the opening of wormholes from which an entire ship can pass."

Aligious continued, "I also said yes to your question because it is not the overall function of the anomaly. It is also the invisible connective signal and identifier for each particle in existence. Oh, of all that is dear, I would like to see a discovery that enables the full visual effect of seeing wormholes in its true form!"

Elijah laughed and asked another question, "Father, the Elders you are meeting with, are their planets in the vicinity of our world and this one?"

"There is a connective simplicity between their worlds and ours," Aligious responded. "The 10 remaining Elders are mostly in the vicinity of the Big Dipper or of Orion's Belt which has been hardwired into all human species whereas other constellations are unnoticed."

Elijah looked interested, so Aligious continued the conversation. "Other programs injected in human DNA are the importance of gold, diamonds, oil and other commodities, even though they are in abundance on Earth. Societies think they're rare, thereby setting the standard for the future. I can brief you at another time on this subject."

"Sure, but please don't forget,"Elijah said. "Are you ready to head back to the Aitho Circle Towers? We can always return here."

As father and son made their way back to the Aitho Towers in the appointed time, Elijah asked Aligious if he can retrieve and research some historical documents while his father is in the meeting and ideas are still fresh in his mind. Aligious agreed and encouraged Elijah to look at Earth's historical findings and the many factions involved with their compromises throughout the millenniums.

Chapter Two

The Meeting

The meeting of the Council of Elders was not going well. Disorganized static was apparent between the Chairs of the Council when a resolution at this juncture of the Earth's development should be reached. The planet's assigned theoretical religious agenda was falling short and headed towards a negative outcome.

Aligious stood up amidst the almost confrontational atmosphere to take control of the discussions. "The juncture that has long ago peaked has reached a point of obvious counter productiveness," he stated.

"The religious undertone and guiding status of all twelve Factions are beginning to conflict because of the increase in other types of agendas," he declared. "We have met a climactic point of stifled growth. I ask you, isn't the whole purpose of our collective works is to eventually have a smooth integration of the human species amongst our own?"

Aligious pointed his index finger to the table and thundered, "Now! Now is the time to take a new measure, conduct a plan that graduates this issue, and introduce a new methodology that allows for change. We need to reestablish once again growth, which is our priority."

He cleared his throat and lowered his voice almost to a whisper, "There should be immediate plans to segue the humans into our respective cultures now. We should not procrastinate; the time is here. Let us conclude this meeting and say that we all agree with one another."

The Council appeared uncomfortable so Aligious continued, "I understand that many of you here feel that we are not ready for a complete integration. Then find a true and decisive way to create an overall shared religion that can bring the many to one, with all the factions and cultures of Earth working together."

Aligious waited a few seconds before he pressed on. "Whether a partial or full believer of what is right and wholesome, people will become united which is a win on all accounts. This can expedite our work with efficiency and increase the population for the integration process."

Each member of the Council started to nod their heads in agreement as Aligious came to an important point. "The pertinent time period to be selected is of utmost importance for success. We, hereby, have to be in unison on our future actions and work together as one."

He halted his speech when one of the Zetas/Grays blurted out, "Why have we not implemented the choice of injecting a supreme religion millennia ago?"

Aligious smiled slightly and remarked, "That's where we will probably go, to the past!"

After the meeting adjourned, certain delegates gathered together as they exited the conference hall. A day passed and the Council unanimously decided to go with Aligious' proposal. The new innovative plan of one religion that pulls all the human factions on earth together will be implemented in an expeditious manner in a specific time period slightly in the past.

As Aligious received the information, many thoughts crossed his mind because it was also announced that it will be his responsibility to carry out the plan.

CHAPTER THREE

ZOBZBALL

It was "Corner Day," the recreational part of the week and very precious to Elijah. On these days, Elijah especially loved to play Zobzball with Aligious. Since their very first game, he had been unable to defeat his father but was always up to the challenge. Elijah was now making his father work for the last few victories.

"Ready and set to play, Elijah?" Aligious put his right hand on Elijah's shoulder to get his attention.

"Ready to engage, sir," Elijah replied with a smile as they headed into the arena.

They entered the Quadratus Arena and walked towards the equipment container to pick up their left- and right-hand racquet gloves, oblong pieces of stranded netting equipment that were slightly bigger than a human hand. The racquet is flush mounted above the palm of the hand. The playing field, itself, looked like a "cube-like court" surrounded by four solid walls of various geometric shapes and sizes that lit up with neon colors and resonated with sound effects when a player hit the ball. It was difficult to anticipate or know the angle of acceleration of a struck ball which was the biggest challenge of the game.

There was a chainlink fence surrounding the court designed to capture or reject a Zobzball. If the fence captured the ball or the ball got wedged in it which was very rare, the player who hit it got a point. If the fence rejected the ball, the ball was magnetically repelled across the playing field to an unknown destination which was a very entertaining part of the game. If the ball went through the fence, it's out of bounds and the player who hit it lost a point.

Suddenly, the crisp rhythm of the Zobzball anthem began while a holographic blue dot appeared in the ceiling's center simulating the looks of a Zobzball and gradually growing larger until it appeared as a 3D holographic structure of a huge score board. Elijah and Aligious looked up to see both their names posted, past stats, and anatomy readings of their bodies.

Aligious backed up, crouching like a sea crab, and yelled, "Your serve!" The player who lost the last time always started as the server. Elijah looked back at his father, snickering at the appearance of his set position, and commanded in a loud voice, "Zobz!"

A Zobzball dropped out from the center of the scoreboard onto the service circle. The game had begun. If the ball hit the ground three times, without hitting any structures, objects, ceiling or walls, the player is awarded a point. Eleven points win a round and two victorious rounds win a match.

Elijah figured out this day that by sending the ball into opposite corners of the cube, it will create a difficult return for Aligious. The many variables that can come out of this type of placement of the ball gave Elijah a valid chance to win. Father and son were tied at one round a piece at the moment with the winner of the next round winning the match which would be a lifetime first for Elijah. There were four points to go for either player and emotions were elevated.

Aligious groaned as he landed a shot high towards the corner ceiling. The ball, with a glancing rebound, floated near both players onto the center of the arena. Aligious was frozen in his stance, anticipating Elijah's new strategic approach of sending the ball into the far corner of the court. However, Elijah faked a shot to the corner and then lightly hit and spun the ball right off Aligious' body unexpectedly, awarding him a point. Aligious let out a moan in frustration as a rumbled sound effect and music erupted from the Zobzball program due to the heightened intensity.

Aligious was the server throughout this final round since Elijah was the winner of the previous round. He served the ball with a double fake and Elijah missed the ball completely. The score was tied again.

Aligious' strength was his wicked fast serve and he used it against Elijah two more times. One more point and Elijah will lose again.

Normally Elijah would be shaken at this point, but he was staying focused. He leaned into Aligious hoping he would hit the ball at the opposite spot of the last serve. He did! Elijah dove face down, alongside his father, and paddled the ball backwards, hitting the ball off the left ankle of Aligious and giving Elijah another point.

Getting ready for the next serve, Elijah moved back and forth, pivoting on the floor so Aligious won't have a bearing on him. Aligious tried to end it fast by smashing a hard shot which flew out of bounds, making it a tied game. One more fault by Aligious and it would lead to Elijah's first ever victory over him. Laughing and sighing, Aligious ran to the service circle and immediately served the ball, trying to catch Elijah off guard while he was not paying attention.

Elijah embraced the moment, stretched his body, and dove to reach for the ball. He missed and as he fell, he felt the breeze of the ball passing by so close. But because Aligious walloped the ball so hard off his racquet, it stayed in play by hitting the tip of one of the geometric shapes. This gave Elijah a second chance to recapture his turn.

Elijah immediately disconnected and released his right-hand racquet off his arm in order to put the palm of his hand flat on the floor, while his body was faced down and falling horizontally to the ground. Gripping the floor with his right hand for lift and support, Elijah sprang up to launch his body back up to a running position and darted across the arena.

Elijah was about to lose the volley because the ball was about to take its third bounce on the floor. His face contorted with an intense look as he concentrated. Quickly, he reattached his racquet while tripping and tumbling towards the ball. Elijah reached with a hyper-extended arm and swept the side of the racquet onto the surface of the floor, slapping a shot upward in the exact center of the fence portion of the Quadratus Arena. Amazingly, the ball wedged perfectly into the middle of the chain-link fence.

Both players froze for what seemed an eternity, wondering if the ball will go through and out of bounds. There was an awkward silence as two seconds went by; both their foreheads crinkled as they stared at the ball. It remained wedged and the final point went to Elijah. Father and son looked at each other stunned, realizing that the young one had finally triumphed. Laughter echoed across the court and blended with the victory music that filled the arena.

Aligious announced, "You have grown and come so far, and look… your name is now in the Winner Circle of the scoreboard!"

Elijah tried to hold a proud and stiff look, then folded and unleashed a laugh as he could not hold it back any longer.

CHAPTER FOUR

BOYHOOD

A strong student with an energetic ambition to forge through his studies, Elijah concluded his cycle in the Erudition School and eagerly awaited the next phase of his education. There were different levels of youth programs starting with Erudition School, then Novitiate Internship, followed by Philosophers Adaptive Stone, then Ministry, and finally Enlightenment. It's a way to help students develop naturally and safely until they reach a pinnacle point of maturity (mainly, the age of twenty-one).

His internship was a long-awaited event in Elijah's life. Some advisors mentioned that Elijah could skip certain aspects of the Novitiate training because he had already accomplished advanced achievements in his youthful state, but he was still stoked about his first day of internship.

He put on his sheer "under garments" that clung to his body. The garments were comprised of a collection of elements that reacted to one's body and temperature, activating microscopic metallic dust particles that fused into the material. The fibers and particles released a residual energy that revitalized cellular tissues, slowing down age and decay.

Elijah finished putting on his full attire and felt a sincere tap on his shoulder. "Come, let us start your long awaited first day," Aligious said.

"Affirmative sir," Elijah responded.

They walked and talked until they reached the lake shore where the Meta Mechin that they will ride was berthed. Aligious proceeded to say, "Once we are actualized at the Meta Mechin, we will be taking a Tube Shuttle and enter an aeronautics facility beneath the earth in the northern hemisphere of the Americas."

Elijah's eyebrows lifted with excitement. "Ready?" asked Aligious. A quick vibrating sound occurred, and the shuttle pierced on through at speeds of hundreds of miles per hour before decelerating and slowly pulling into an open hangar of immense size as far as the eyes can see. They had reached the Tube Shuttle Complex beneath a lake.

Aligious looked over at his son and smiled upon witnessing the expression on his face. Elijah was overwhelmed by the dreamlike atmosphere: colorful lights throughout the whole compound, computer circuitry in workstations, shiny glass rock ceilings, ship platforms, holographic glass monitors, and a vast display of different vessels.

Elijah asked his father a question while the Tube Shuttle dropped off other passengers in transit. "Where do we get off?"

Aligious suddenly shifted forward in his seat and appeared as if they had reached "their" stop at the facility, extending his neck while the shuttle came to an abrupt turn. Elijah sensed his father's movement, turned to look up as they turn the final corner, and saw a large and very real replica of the vessel that he had only seen as a toy during his childhood years.

Emotions filled Elijah as he viewed the "Bit-Cargo" submersible freighter staring back at him peacefully. "This is great," he exclaimed with a gracious glance to his father.

Father and son disembarked from the Tube Shuttle and Aligious began explaining the different parts of the ship and how the vehicle works and the importance of its uses while walking around the vessel. The chief engineer and the mechanics were almost done with the vehicle, making sure it was ready for departure.

Elijah noticed a Zeta (Grey) and an Earth-human working together, a first for him. He remembered the secrecy doctrine, assuming that the human had probably sworn the important oath. Elijah was curious and desired to interact with the human to ask questions. He wanted to find out if the person had conflicts about this systemic Earth operation.

His thoughts were broken when Aligious entered the craft and beckoned him to follow. Aligious sat at the back of the vehicle and pointed towards an area high above the rear of the ship. "Can you see those bars with blue lights leading down from the ceiling far apart from one another, having a similar design to the Meta Mechin?" he yelled while heavy machinery ran close by,

"Yes, they appear to be a larger version of the Meta Mechin Gate," Elijah replied. "We are going to travel through that gate, are we not?"

"Indeed," replied Aligious. "There will be two separate actions of reversed time when we launch. As we depart and release from the Meta Gate inside this facility, there will also be a Meta Gate receiving us from the other side. We will be exiting out of the twin Meta Gate at the bottom of Lake Groom many years back in time."

Elijah stroked the alloy on the ship, sliding his hand along the curves of the vessel as he settled inside the vessel. He began to knock on the vehicle's frame to get the feel of the graphein anodic material from which the ship is made.

From inside the ship, Aligious announced, "Here we go!" Elijah fell back into one of the two front seats near the control panel in a state of wonder and savored the moment.

Aligious moved to an observational position in the ship and began to explain the operations of the vehicle. He overlooked the already programmed coordinates and tapped the glass controls while he pivoted in his seat. He then faced Elijah and said, "Undoubtedly you are aware of the efforts by the Unity of Councils in recent times. I have been put in charge and in a position to oversee major important functions."

"Elijah, these functions must be finished exactly and according to specifications," he continued. "Please understand the importance of certain procedures that are involved with temporal displacements or when time travels are involved. It is paramount to whoever is in charge to follow strict and mathematical orders with all procedures!"

Elijah nervously nodded once, replied with a resounding "yes," and then nodded once more with a serious stare.

Aligious changed his demeanor and put his right hand and arm around part of his son's chair then said, "Eli, just to let you know, we are going to be traveling to Earth's satellite."

Elijah quickly replied, "The Mene?" His mood immediately lightened, and he quickly understood his father's authoritative stance earlier.

Aligious uttered, "Yes the (Mene) Moon, but the new Moon."

Elijah questioned, "New?"

Aligious engaged the protective field at the outer part of the ship and explained, "Well, to start, let me cite a quote from a book I have read, called, "The Later Part of the Moon." "Paradox in a bemused way, it is our quest to travel eons into the past. We went back approximately 4.5 billion years ago to create the inception of the Moon's construct."

Aligious cocked his right brow directly to Elijah, then looked ahead. Elijah reacted, looked forward and realized that the ship was currently in motion, rising high up to the ceiling of the facility. A soothing hum filled the vehicle. They were now hovering right in front of the Meta Transgate.

Stunned, Elijah sat back in silence, acknowledging the ship's ability to move with slight noise, along with no motion shifting. He was quiet and transfixed on the Transgate, staring, and thinking about traveling through the water and far back in time.

Aligious said to Elijah, "Let's just enjoy the journey and I will brief you thoroughly once we have arrived at our destination. Are you ready to get on?"

Elijah fidgeted with his posture and delivered a sincere, "Yes sir."

Instantly, a bright azure horizontal light flashed across the Transgate and Elijah was breathless as he observed the ship's position. The ship was immediately on a forty-degree angular ascent, propelling swiftly and silently through the ancient lake and its fresh waters. Submerged in the water, Elijah crinkled his nose and was amazed by the feeling of stability. It was like he was sitting at home.

The interior of the ship had no movement at all, even though the freighter was traveling very fast and on an obscure trajectory angle. The day was becoming more interesting and impressive for Elijah, with more expected to follow.

Aligious often glanced over at Elijah, taking great joy in seeing his son filled with happiness. The water was undisturbed as they fly smoothly, not a single bubble nor a wave, making Elijah more curious.

The ship was rapidly approaching the surface of the lake. Elijah was looking up and out of the window, enjoying the motion effects of the sea, when a volume of light suddenly engulfed the vehicle as the ship left the water into the sunlight.

On their ascending approach to the sky, Elijah looked back down at the lake, appreciating the reflections and glistening water that looked like sprinkled diamonds dancing across the veneer of Groom Lake. The ship flew away, whipping itself into the proper longitude and latitude coordinates, and self-maneuvering with the pre-positioned system location that was previously programmed.

A journey of this magnitude had to be formed with a two-step process for safety and exactitude. The first was a minor time jump into the past from a preselected time period. The second step included setting up a major destination that's chosen because of the considerable leap back in time. At the moment, Aligious and Elijah were crossing over to a particular time period billions of years in the past.

CHAPTER FIVE

THE MOON

Hovering high in the sky with all marks and functions fully engaged, father and son were about to travel back in time approximately four and a half billion years ago. They would exit the wormhole at an approximate distance, arriving between the Earth and its Moon.

Aligious started the countdown and cried out, "Engage!"

Their vessel quickly occupied volumes of dimensional space and hummed, entering the barrier of the wormhole. Time slowly became displaced as silence filled the interior of the ship. Elijah experienced not only the silence but a paralysis and numbness of his senses, experiencing a type of floating sensation.

Suddenly, a sound of shuttered noise passed which was followed by a suction dense pop, leaving the vessel still and peaceful in space. Aligious checked the status and saw they had successfully arrived at their destination between the Moon and the Earth, hovering steady in space.

"Well, well, we have arrived!" Aligious turned to Elijah, using those familiar terms to his son during moments of magnitude and excitement such as this.

"Will we do that again?" Elijah replied. "I mean, when we go back, will we be using the same method for our return?"

Aligious laughed then replied, "Actually, we will be residing here for quite some time in a subterranean technologically advanced city called Columbia. It is located on the far-side of the satellite or the infamous Dark Side of the Moon."

Aligious gave a hearty laugh at this iconic phrase before changing his demeanor to a more serious one. "Eli, why don't you move about the ship because we are going to stay docked at these coordinates for a short duration of time. Come and enjoy the full view."

 The ship's windows revealed a backdrop view of the Universe, Galaxies, and the Earth's solar system. Elijah suddenly noticed an oddity about the Moon's surface, glancing back and forth from the Moon to the Earth to the Sun. "Father, I understand why the younger Earth has these black and molten veins," he stated. "It is due to its infant stage and of course the Sun is intact as it should be, but the Moon; it has a silvery type of surface and appears to have geometric pentagonal patterns?"

Elijah was about to mimic a phrase from an old popular nursery rhyme but decided he had better not and stymied his humor. He realized he was now an intern in a serious and most important project.

Aligious headed back to his seat and told Elijah, "To best answer your question, we should travel into the planetary system of Mars. Brace yourself since we are about to charge up some astronomical speeds, no pun intended."

Aligious grunted a rough laugh while he powered up the control panel. "I am going to slightly decelerate the motion safety field so we can experience a genuine speed sensation," he said.

Elijah smiled and enjoyed the 33 million miles of shooting, spinning and sharp aggressive turns in space, having a great moment of solidarity with his father. The journey would create a new fond memory between father and son.

While traveling through the asteroid belt, they engaged the Bessel Tractor Beam that locks onto matter in space by means of magnetism photonics. Aligious fiddled in his seat while he steered the ship at high speeds in angled position, grabbing and tossing asteroid rocks with the beam.

Elijah laughed as the ship turned and maneuvered between the debris. He shared with his father how thrilling the experience was and how he enjoyed it just as much as playing Zobzball. It sparked a great appreciation towards his father in Elijah that he yearned to give back.

They came to an abrupt halt after reaching their mark, and Aligious turned serious. "I have purposely situated us in an orbit around Mars so I can explain this saga to you and the oddity about the Earth's Moon."

"The planets and moons that inhabit this solar system were deemed to be barren and fruitless, with no chance of any intelligent life," he began. "These findings were based upon the reports of the Time Flexion Unit, a multi-faction security team that monitors activities in all sectors of the galaxy."

"The Factions initiated actions to supply life where there is none. Their core belief is that the basis of our existence is about giving life."

Elijah interrupted, "Isn't there a conflict of the moral understanding that life is solely predicated by the Prime Creator, unto itself?"

Aligious explained, "As our species developed, the challenge amongst ourselves, as well as the Factions, is not to abuse the gifts of life the Creator has bestowed upon us all but to embellish it. Unfortunately, there is no clear unity between the Factions, past or present, when spawning new life all should have an absolute oneness."

Aligious stared at Elijah and said, "The Factions amongst the Council are the ones I am in charge of currently. We're not always unified but nevertheless, we strive to work together. Life was created where there was none."

Aligious' eyes glazed over. Elijah thought to himself that his father had mixed feelings about what he was going to say. "Understandingly, there is a moral debate but let's hold that aside as of now," he intoned. "Please, Elijah, like most information given to you, don't conclude or judge till you have heard the complete history."

"To answer your original question about the silvery look to the Moon, let me tell you that the Moon that orbits the Earth is a manufactured object!"

Elijah was visibly confused as the monitor started displaying the construction process of the Earth's Moon. He watched as the Earth's molten lava was transferred to the Moon's surface and fused to a metal caging in pentagonal sections. Inside, it resided cities for different necessities and functions with exits and entrances on the far side of the moon that allow spacecraft access for fueling and maintenance.

"The facility bases on the Moon are one of many stations that are inhabited by beings throughout this solar system. With regards to the facility bases, second to Earth is Mars which was a full functioning base for reconnaissance missions," Aligious continued.

Elijah was now curious on what happened on Mars and why the Factions are only present on Earth. He asked why there is such an abundance of life on Earth compared to other planets he had monitored.

"The Factions designed the plans for Earth's satellite according to what research and development say have the optimum potential for life," Aligious explained. "We created the moon to fit into 1/4 of the circumference of the Earth, along with intentionally making the Moon 1/400 of the circumference of the Sun, from the perspective on Earth. These series of mathematical ratios regarding the relationship of the Earth, Sun and Moon are paramount to produce an exuberant amount of life."

"I have heard of a published literary story entitled, 'Eclipsed by the Moon,' discussed at my Erudition School on how popular the Earth's Moon is amongst the Factions," Elijah mentioned.

Aligious nodded and added, "The Earth's Moon's best feature and unique unto itself is the uncanny ability to slightly rotate slowly at a fixed speed to precisely and constantly face the Earth, allowing the inhabitants of Earth to see only one side. This unnatural occurrence is how the Factions maintain a surreptitious behind-the-scenes covert operation on the far-side (dark side) of the Moon."

"I will now tell you about the tragedy on Mars," Aligious carried on. "Portions of the planet flourished with acceptable life and water, but the rest of the planet is non-fertile. The project to make it productive caused and created controversy with the different Factions involved and not involved in the project, and some Faction Leaders became upset that they were not chosen. Those excluded from the base facility development led a violent war, sixty-six thousand plus years ago, in and around Mars."

The onslaught was devastating, spreading nuclear and electromagnetic annihilation over a large portion of the planet. Consequently, an ample quantity of life was transferred, saved, or destroyed, sending the planet practically back to its previous original lifeless state. The fabricated moon for Mars was obliterated thus halting the replenishment of life. Its destruction became a reminder for all to protect life at any costs.

"The war had paved the way for the founding of the Unification of Planets with a fair and equal twelve-part Faction alliance," continued Aligious. "New projects would now include all the various factions, along with certain territorial locations for hybrid development in the case of Earth. Every Faction was given an allotted section on Earth, designated solely for them."

The Heads of the Factions taught their own special knowledge from languages and writing capabilities to mathematical skills. The final leg of the process, and the most necessary, was the installation of religions. Many of the religions were carefully selected and quite similar to a particular Faction's historic religion in their home planet.

Unfortunately, certain hybrid Earth Faction leaders botched their religious programs. Many of them used technology to impress the humans so as to be worshipped, which was unacceptable. Another unacceptable practice was doing excessive experimentation due to scientific obsession, believing it will lead to dominance.

Elijah asked why people did not challenge or question anything and Aligious replied, "Son, the people on earth are quite intelligent that's why it is hard for me to understand how their species does not question the most obvious oddities. They accept things at face value."

Aligious took a deep breath and said, "Well, let's go back to the Moon at a faster pace, what do you say?"

Elijah responded with a positive gesture of agreement, then said, "Nevertheless, I know there is an underlying human seriousness that we must recognize."

Aligious gave a light gasp with a short laugh then listened.

"Father, I now see that my energies would best be served by studying human languages, writings and religions," Elijah continued. "Hopefully, I can help speed up the process so people will not suffer anymore or be herded like cattle in the name of science."

Aligious told Elijah, "You're starting to sound like me, ha ha. Why don't you take the helm and let's make our way back to the Earth's Moon?"

Elijah's expression lit up and he gathered himself to control the ship, asking his father if he can use the manual steering during the trip back. Aligious agreed and they set off to return to the Moon.

Many months went by with Elijah and his father living in the Columbian city, getting into a rhythmic enjoyable way of life. They were busy with the Lunar Housing Development Project which was almost finished with great assistance and innovative influence from Elijah.

Aligious was proud and grateful when his son's internship concluded. He was filled with great honor during his son's graduation because of the high levels achieved by Elijah.

Elijah knew how pleased his father was and was joyful as he gathered his belongings. He had to leave his father behind to finish the Moon construct. He understood it was his time to move on and travel alone to the space station within the quadrants of his father's home planet.

Chapter Six

Historic Data Machine

The rite of passage was upon Elijah. He was about to receive an amazing amount of knowledge from a machine, using artificial intelligence. The Philosopher Adaptive Stone contained an assortment of information from the Factions' past histories, current cultures, languages, actions, and writings.

What was withdrawn from the historic documents in the apparatus was any portion of history that the receiver was connected to. Information relative to someone's future was not included in the transfer. This precaution ensured that history will not be affected, nor the time continuum. Nonetheless, the program won't be installed until the user had reached maturity and qualified.

Since Elijah had accomplished some of the most significant outcomes for his age, extra care would be taken. The Time Flexion Security was assigned to monitor his life. He had the highest level of security and was tracked through an inter-dimensional monitoring system.

While waiting in the prep area, Elijah stared into the main room and relaxed as he cleared his mind. He was administered a series of medicines to prevent info-overlapping then walked into a ziggurat stone-shaped structure which he realized was carved from one enormous stone.

Elijah gulped as he saw the circular platform on which he was supposed to stand, knowing he would lose consciousness. There were field barriers that would keep him in a residual standing position during the procedure.

He walked slowly noticing blue and green lighted reactors connected to some sort of cylindrical canisters, housing tall thin obelisk crystals. Approaching the center of the room, he looked down to see the wireless mechanical transponders. There were four recessed wireless transponders smoothened on the floor's surface.

Before he engaged with the Philosopher Stone, Elijah received instructions from the professional staff at hand. Various professionals briefed him and explained the process on how to breathe during the procedure. They reassured and reminded him that the area of the mind that would be utilized was only 1% of his entire capacity.

Elijah smiled, nodded, and stepped completely onto the cylindrical platform as the staff operators moved away to a range of twenty feet. Elijah waited and before he connected, a sudden spherical force field dome encompassed him. Running high levels of pressurized oxygen, the four floor transponders were directed towards different parts of Elijah's cranium.

Each of the four transponders had a task: the first balanced the bio-chemical reactants to keep the process on a safe forward path. The second transponder produced and stimulated neurotransmitters while the third one fused the neuron receptors to the incoming information. The fourth transponder embedded the data permanently in the receiver's memory.

The arduous procedure finished, and Elijah was drowsy, docile and in a meditative state. The team monitored him, adjusted nutrients, and allowed him to rest and recover.

After the third day, Elijah started feeling better and contemplated all the new information. He was beside himself with the knowledge of hundreds of lifetimes. Strangely enough, Elijah's first thought was of a regenerative bath where flowers, herbs and oils are in the bath waters that pulsate with a low voltage magnetic massage.

Elijah realized this was one of the reasons why the Centurion Faction was able to live for a few centuries. "Maybe that's why we are called Centurions," he thought. Then he immediately drew a blank memory signifying that his previous thought had no merit.

Elijah smiled as he looked up with a glazed expression, turned his body to the right in a circular slow motion, hands and palms opened face up, and saw things as though everything was transparent, and he was grateful.

Elijah made an observation and came to a conclusion to tie everything together. He switched thoughts immediately and wondered about the barriers that had held the human race from accelerating beyond their capabilities. His thoughts tussled in a search for answers on how to help the people of Earth.

Ignorant on how to put this into action, he spurred a thought and came to the realization that the humans were given religions that they diligently worshiped, but overall did not understand what they were worshiping. They were just doing what they were told by their parents, peers, and leaders.

Every day that passed, more conclusions reached him, enhancing his already outstanding intellect and personality. The answer was religion, and it was the only solution. The question must be asked, how do you decipher the best exact time to implement and teach this religion? Understandably, it would be in a non-technological era, sometime in the remote past.

Elijah, after considerable contemplation over a period of time, was determined to set out one day to start his own ministry and through his love and actions spark a religion that would both accelerate and bring together mankind as one.

CHAPTER SEVEN

EIGHT-YEAR MINISTRY

Time was fleeing and Elijah was busy preparing for his ministry, learning a vivid way to walk with righteousness and grace, and to talk with forgiveness and words that bring divine results. He understood that the people were burdened with sin and the rigidness of Earth's challenges that hinder their ability to evolve over a long period of time.

This work in progress was classified under a genome study titled Stranded Identification Nucleases (SIN) which installed beliefs in the connection between Satan/Lucifer and sin (SIN Personified). What was originally a genetic program to advance human evolution morphed into a psychological conditioning campaign based on fear so mankind will behave better.

Yet societies did not move in an acceptable direction because the guidelines of change and moral standards were compromised. It was decided to implement certain revolting choices because of the immense volume of problems (DNA Infractions).

The Zetas (Grays) had directed plagues to geographic areas of choice in the past to tame and limit cantankerous populations while controlling DNA adjustments. It led to the demise of hundreds of millions of people on Earth but soon after, a new agreement limited the Zetas to a ten-year window of inducing diseases and of monitoring/studying. It led to a better methodology and techniques for boosting DNA advancements, with the cure to follow.

Elijah tried hard to understand the Zetas' analytics on human genome for he was bitter on many accounts. One in particular was the various diseases installed directly into the original design of the human DNA which the Zetas can activate and at any point in an individual's life for analytical studies.

Elijah learned that when an individual becomes infected, a case study was opened and activated using a bio-frequency monitoring system. The Zetas utilized the technology to observe how the individual behaved, along with family behavior and reactions.

There was also important data that detailed how the body reacts and fights the disease while monitoring the will to survive, coupled with results from medications. The results were factored into adjusting and strengthening the DNA to advance the evolutionary track of mankind.

Overstepping their authority, the Zetas had employed a time temporal device in certain instances that took data results from the future. They used the device to eliminate people who did not match the required standards of the new world. In effect, they targeted innocent individuals for elimination by activating diseases.

Elijah processed this information and contemplated what will be the best approach for all that is to come.

Mission

Elijah had to choose a time period for his mission wherein the results would be most productive and worthy of a religious movement. This was of utmost importance and he turned to his superiors for guidance.

Dealing with his superiors was quite a challenge, but they agreed to place Elijah in 9th century BC or the post King Solomon Era. It was a time when the kingdoms were divided, with the Kingdom of Judah in the south and the Kingdom of Israel in the north ruled by Omri.

Omri had a son, Ahab, who eventually became the ruler of the Northern Territory. Ahab married the daughter of the King of Sidon in Phoenicia, who worshiped the foreign god Baal. Ahab, looking to accelerate idol worship, implored his wife to convince the masses to the greatness of the god Baal. The couple enticed the tribes from outside their country to join them on a quest of economic and spiritual bliss.

Elijah concluded that Ahab's ratchet narcissism deluded him into believing he was Baal. As Baal, he portrayed himself before the people as a god, exploiting their ignorance and receiving their worship.

Elijah knew exactly what to do and confidently addressed Ahab and the people and told them, "There will be years of drought upon this land, for the people of the land need to be reconciled."

Once it commenced, Elijah left the land and met with his superiors who advised him to take care of the innocent and to ensure that they will not be affected by the modified weather in selected locations. He was provided by his superiors with a Manna device that produced food from simplistic elements to feed and assist the needy.

Elijah gave it to a lady whose village lacked food, and she shared it with many of her people. But at the same moment, the woman's son died suddenly, and the timing of her son's death and the appearance of the odd Manna machine roused her suspicion. She questioned Elijah and held him responsible.

Elijah conversed with the elders and a decision was made. "Do what you feel is right. You no longer have to consult with us," he was told. Elijah was granted carte blanche because of his trustworthiness, positive traits, and decision-making abilities.

Elijah returned to the lady and explained very little. He knelt alongside the woman's son and slowly pushed away the hair on the son's forehead. Elijah's hand lied flat over the child's eyes while the mother was on her knees repenting her sins and quivering in prayer.

Elijah concentrated to increase the nimbus energy that emanated from his spirit. He transferred a dynamic aura of veracity around the boy, causing the boy's own spirit to be retrieved, swayed in a magnetized direction back to the body, and joined an already healed body.

The child was revived, (this was the first known raising of the dead by a prophet) and the mother hysterically thanked Elijah. "Whatever can I do, whatever can I do for you?" she cried.

Elijah responded clearly, "All the people should worship Yahweh, which is the one and only God, not an idol, rather the creator of heaven and of these worlds. Today you have seen and believed but since the Creator cannot be seen, your faith will be your sight and your heart will build your love for him and each other. This will be done!" Elijah reassured the mother with a warm smile before he departed.

Elijah moved on to various regions and spread the teachings of the "one God," successfully bringing together the troubled tribes. He shared certain techniques and special skills to numerous tribes, but only one technique and skill per tribe, so that each of the tribes had to share and trade with the others.

After three years of drought and turmoil, Elijah returned to Ahab and his Kingdom. Upon arrival, Elijah found many people of good faith who adhered to what he spoke of three years prior, "the belief in one God."

Yet, there was no change in the heart of Ahab and his ways. Elijah realized that the king was going to continue being stubborn and without contrition. Trying something new, Elijah attempted to challenge Ahab in a contest of action and wit, but the latter refused.

Announcing the three-year drought over, Elijah saw that he had captured the old, devoted believers and did not need to sway Ahab. Majority of the tribes and followers overcame the worship of Baal and devoted themselves to believing in one God, "Yahweh."

CHAPTER EIGHT

THE QUIETUS

Elijah traveled on foot alongside the River Jordan, heading to his next and last mission with only thirty days left. Silence surrounded him and he appreciated the beauty of the water. Walking relaxed, he was suddenly drawn to a reflection in the sky of a vehicle of some sort. Appearing in the distance was a man coming towards him.

As the man got closer, Elijah recognized Elisha, his replacement a month ago. He could see that Elisha looked uneasy and there was something wrong. Elijah greeted Elisha nervously and muttered, "What's wrong?"

Elisha answered, "Elijah, your father was found not well, drifting in his vessel in an odd area in space, out of our region. Aligious was discovered by a stranger that is not of this sector. This is all I could gather because of the difficulty in the time positioning sensors, I am sorry."

Elijah gazed down while he recited an old prayer in his mind. Elisha continued, "I have brought the only ship that I could find immediately, so you can get to your father as soon as you can. I will stay here and take care of the rest of your works, and they have been wonderful works, Elijah."

Elijah's throat constricted as he barely got out a, "Thank you." The ship hovered high waiting for his command. Elijah signaled the hover ship to a clear pickup point, and a beam of light surrounded him. He made eye contact with Elisha as he ascended into the vessel, with a serious stare in the manner of a prayer.

Just a few days ago, a space time continuum alarm sounded for the Time Flexion Security Team. The security team was on alert and in place to respond to any time disturbance. A flash of energy suddenly appeared on their monitor and they initiated an immediate pursuit. They intercepted a foreign vessel pyramidical in appearance and not familiar to them.

The security team began to cross-reference all possible vehicles in its database and was unable to find a match. Scanning the visitor's ship, the team detected two life readings, one a Centurion and the other unknown. (Elijah would later learn that the stranger who rescued his father was from the Andromeda Galaxy who saw Aligious' vessel drifting.) The security team attempted to hail the ship but before they could do so, the foreign vessel sent a request to communicate.

The message was to the point. "Aligious is not well and found unconscious, adrift in his vessel very far from his observatory mark." Aligious was nearing the final stages of his three hundred seventy-six-year-old life, signifying the end of the unpredictable Centurion lifespan. This was known as the "Quietus," an activated transition of the spirit energy's inability to cling on to the physical body.

Aligious, unfortunately, was in the last stages of the Quietus, unable to talk because of the limited bodily functions during the final transformation/departure. There was only a small window of opportunity for Elijah to see his father, who meant everything to him. Elijah was rushing but it was becoming evident that Elijah had little or no time left before Aligious' sacred transitioning.

Word had spread throughout the sector that the last hour of Aligious had begun. Multitudes of people were outside the dwelling, amongst them heads of states from different sectors who patiently waited to support Elijah during this Quietus.

Elijah, in flight, accelerated the ship to hypersonic speed before slamming the field engines in reverse as the ship fell sideways in a drift. He then immediately popped the vehicle back into forward acceleration, forcing it to whip ahead in a stable safe level of control. Elijah successfully arrived and slingshot the craft to his old dwelling, alerted to the fact that crowds of people were on the grounds.

He came to a quiet halt above the place and lowered his vehicle to the side of the dwelling. Elijah looked out the window as he shut down the vehicle and was taken back as he saw the droves of people lining the grounds. He was flabbergasted by the number of people gathered to pay their respects.

Elijah settled the ship as close to the house as possible and exited the vehicle. He passed a portion of the crowd as he approached the front entryway. Heads of Factions saluted him and patted his shoulders as he fell to numbness. He entered the dwelling somber and solo, his eyes blurry with tears as he moved seemingly in slow motion towards his father.

Elijah saw the light particles hovered and slowly recollected above his father's still body, and he let out a choked sob. He looked down at his father and slid his hand underneath his father's clasped hands. He grasped the right hand of Aligious, holding it tight.

With a knee on the floor, Elijah pressed his father's hand against his heart. It was holding on for dear life and Elijah knew these were the last moments. He mustered out the broken words, "I want, will be, like you, you are everything. Promise to keep you close, all to my heart, will promise to give, all because of you. I'll make you proud with love."

Elijah was suddenly moved by the glorious radiance gleaming around Aligious. He rose from his knee and stood hunched over the sparkling light, realizing that his father's spiritual aura was no longer within his body. He stretched his hand to reach out for the luminescence and said his final words to his father. "Choose paradise, Father, I will miss you and hold you here," Elijah sobbed, tapping his fist against his heart. As Elijah's teardrops disappeared into the dissolving remaining light, so did his father. Thus, the "Quietus" was over.

Whilst the spirit is being called to the afterlife, it is known amongst the Centurions as the "Revivification Passing."

Chapter Nine

Ministry Conclusion

Elijah's ministry was from 852 BC to 860 BC (Old Testament), one year beyond his required stay in the territory. He started with the work of Moses and other prophets somewhat undone. The Elders were in agreement and extremely frustrated, but Elijah's ministration did steer the sector back on track for the moment.

It was a known fact that the world would need thousands of Elijah/s to keep a sustainable order. Elijah thought there must be a better way. He prayed, "Oh, dear God, what can be done to keep the people on track without them straying away?"

In the present day, there are various religions that recognize this great prophet for his teachings and his monumental accomplishments. Elijah was a whirlwind of action with numerous miracles performed like controlling the weather, multiplying food, countless healing of the sick, and strengthening the family unit.

Elijah's list of outstanding miracles includes:

Shut the heavens and stopped rain for three years (1 Kings 17:1)

Oil multiplied and grain increased daily for the widow woman (1 Kings 17:2)

Widow's son raised from the dead (1 Kings 17:22, 23)

Fire from heaven on the soaked altar (1 Kings 18:38)

Rain returned (1 Kings 18:45)

Fire brought down on the 51 soldiers (2 Kings 1:10)

Fire brought down on the next 51 soldiers (2 Kings 1:12)

The parting of the River Jordan (2 Kings 2:8)

Elijah's life is noted in history (Old Testament only) as the ministry of the "Wonder Worker." He is noted as one of the greatest prophets that ever lived, but as the future unfolds, he became one of the most influential people in the history of humankind!

It has been said that Aligious was the architect of the "Old Testament" while the Dead Sea scrolls and fragments point to Elijah as responsible for the "New Testament." His relationship to Jesus/Yeshua as a mentor goes far beyond the original writings.

The fragments from "The Book of Elijah" have been understandably omitted (withheld) from the New Testament but as the future unfolds, they reveal the connection between the Old and New Testaments as one and the same!

"They as a species have learned that the deficiency or neutrality sense of behavior in ones' life, fuels no energy to the spirits' passage. The conscious actions, thoughts and decisions that have a positive result is the heart & betterment of a wide array of all things in the spirit's choice. He, who has the will to thrust that spirit, yet not unto an aesthetic distance, but with the discretionary love and divinity, is to elevate choices for ones' sequential destiny." – Elijah

Chapter Ten

Cave Innovation

Aligious' death upset Elijah greatly that he went back to Judah in the distant past for a journey of spiritual cleansing, traveling the desert for forty days. This pilgrimage was something that Elijah was not required to do, unlike many other prophets, because he was gifted. The Elders wanted him to start his ministry as soon as he completed the school for Prophesiers.

Without notifying anyone, Elijah journeyed to a specific time period only known to him in the rocky and barren Judaean Desert. After being gone for three days, the Elders tracked his whereabouts without alerting him of their presence. On the morning of the thirtieth day, the guardians had to intercede and placed bread with water beside him every morning until the fortieth day was completed. This was the practice for all Prophets/Seers during their journey of divine spiritual cleansing in the desert.

Finishing the final days of his pilgrimage, Elijah began to think how concerned the Elders were with his well-being that they searched for him in order to supply him with nourishment. He had a flashback to when his father told him a story.

"If I tended to a large flock of sheep and one of the herds was lost, would I search for that one even though I have so many?" Aligious said. "There will be more joy over one sinner who repents and returns, than many righteous people who need no repentance."

At the end of Elijah's pilgrimage, he steered his way to the grotto entrance at Mount Horeb. On this cave near the summit was where Moses received the Ten Commandments milleniums ago. It was an old facility where his father had worked and shared some of his experiences with Elijah a long time ago.

Elijah meandered his way to the old genetics' facility base called "Sinai." He was very familiar with the facility though, by and large, it had become an abandoned, vast empty space with the exception of a small area in the complex that was used as a monitoring station.

Exhausted, Elijah's left leg buckled, and his knee landed on the sand. He then placed his right elbow crossed onto his top thigh, leaning on his bent perpendicular right leg. He rested his face in the palm of his hand and prayed, "Father, who is heaven, ask God if I can receive the goodness of *(His)* Glory and the Greatness of *(His)* Graces, thy will it, please!"

Elijah felt a tear rolled pass his cheek towards the right side of his chin. He heard the soft tap of transparent drops as the grains of sand received a cascade of sorrow. Suddenly, a ray of sunlight reappeared from behind a cloud, casting a shimmering appeal to the wet specks of sand and reminding the young prophet of his father's Quietus.

"Worrying is just a poor way of praying," he could hear Aligious saying. Elijah was filled with a strong feeling of nostalgia and remembered what his father said when he was younger, "You can throw all your sins into the depths of the sea and God will forgive you. God forgives all our sins except for one. If you do not repent, you cannot have forgiveness."

Elijah entered the chamber that will lead him to his old quarters. In the corridors he was passing through, there were different rooms with stacks of technological parts and materials. He was intrigued and stopped to look at some of the laboratories.

Finally, Elijah reached his stateroom from long ago located at the rear of the facility. Upon opening the door, he saw that everything was more or less intact as it was left all those years ago. Now that his father was gone, he was inundated with feelings of loneliness.

Elijah's thoughts crossed to the idea that the current religious movement was lacking effectiveness because of the many inconsistencies. He realized that it was no longer adequate to use holographic imagery or resort to controlling the weather to win over the hearts of humans. Fear or magic was no longer effective. He prayed, "I will persevere to find the answers and I am here in Your presence, oh God, so that I may do Your will."

Elijah quickly adapted into a daily routine inside the facility. At sunrise, he headed to the cuisine counter of the monitoring station which read and scanned individual anamorphic anatomy and automatically prepared food to bring the body up to optimum level. This efficient dieting was what Elijah was lacking ever since his father's Quietus.

Elijah loved to rummage through the compound gathering any material that was interesting to him and bringing it back to the most advanced laboratory. He lined up the items and categorized each and every part of his collection. He often found himself taking apart and searching for certain significant components in abandoned crafts for hours. It was a brutal regimented work schedule with long arduous days.

Historical Data

Elijah's spirits were the highest they have been in a while now that he was focused. He was fascinated with certain eras in time such as when the twelve Factions agreed to distribute their own DNA throughout the geographical land they were assigned to. From this "Planetary Union" agreement came the special blend of DNA which became the foundation of the Human-Kind Species inhabiting Earth.

Elijah came upon a list of the Factions' choices of DNA and geographical locations on Earth:

Centurion	Primate	Faction	Location
FOXP2	27GTTGG	ZETA	ASIA
FOXP2	6OBPP/GWGG	ELDS	AFRICA

FOXP2	TCSO68	ANILIANS	INDIA
FOXP2.	6MSCS4	CETIANS	S. EUROPE
FOXP2	RZCPK14	ARCHURIANS	N. EUROPE
FOXP2	TGG45	PELEIDIANS	PN. ISLANDS
FOXP2	7CBCF29	SIRAINS	BALTIC
FOXP2	LBTLC5.	RENDIANS	C. AMERICA
FOXP2	IPMMP29	MINTAKAS	N. AMERICA
FOXP2	4RKK	NAZCANS	S. AMERICA
FOXP2	LBTLC831	ANNUNAKI	MIDDLE EAST
FOXP2	29PBP	CENTURIONS	AUSTRALIAN

Elijah mused that it was going to be a very difficult to bring all the different cultures and ethnicity to one religious outcome. Measures that were taken from the extreme past proved ineffective that removal of past civilizations were done through an ice-age, floods, and plagues.

Elijah sneered at a note attached to the historic documents, claiming that the people in these tragedies did not die in vain. It stated that they were contributory to the event and was an important part of the natural history of Earth that helped mankind developed into what they became. Yet Elijah couldn't help thinking that the people should have been relocated to live out the remaining years of their lives, instead of enduring unacceptable fierce deaths.

Elijah pondered that it stands to reason why humans are attracted to prayer in order to live. He contemplated, "Wouldn't it be wonderful to take prayer as a physical as well as conscious continuity with the Creator? How do I make that connection? How can I equate the best and greatest outcome? I need to visualize."

Elijah stopped mid-thought and remembered a moment from his childhood when his father brought him to a dwelling completion ceremony. He witnessed the communion ritual between his father and the workers, sharing bread, drinking wine, and pouring dabs of that wine on the inscribed cornerstone. He remembered the speech clearly.

"To the bread that nourishes our bodies, to the particles of all who has lived and of the wine that replenishes our heartening souls. As to a far nobler harmonious life, onward to creating equality and gratitude of which is to come. Live as one with-all!" - Elijah

Innovation

Also from the same ceremony, Aligious said "Certain things can't be seen, but can be visualized." Elijah jumped up from his reminiscing and connected with his father's quote, figuring that the unseen such as wormholes, magnetic fields and other invisible manifestations can be measured and detected by field sensors. He got excited as he realized it was the key to successfully creating a divine connection. To see what can't be seen.

"Everything invented has been reinvented 99.9% of the time, but necessary for all times."- Aligious

Convex Spectacles

Elijah was now focused on making a visual apparatus to see what cannot be seen. He was attempting to create a non-invasive bio-electric frequency signal that is a couple of inches above the bridge of the nose, on a pair of goggle-like spectacles. Elijah strongly feels the apparatus could be the key to the connectivity of the almighty creative force or even possibly God *(Allah, Elohim, Yahweh, Jehovah)*.

Elijah pondered that the sensory input from the user's eyes can be combined with the modified sensory systems for thoughts and emotions, as well as the auditory cortex for sound absorption. This paired structure is the major component that must work as one with the lens field in order to produce the image.

Elijah went to work, plugging into the central computer, connecting the transponders, and testing for brain functions until the lenses were ready for activation. He was finally ready to test the Convex Spectacles, the name given later on by someone other than Elijah to his invention.

Elijah powered up the glasses, placed them over his eyes, and turned on the appropriate engagement triggers. He chose from a pre-list of anomalies to see the signatures of oxygen atoms. He paused briefly and asked for a blessing.

As Elijah began to open his eyes, he started to spin slowly and quickly noticed a blur. He then used the cylindrical manual adjuster on the right metal ocular frame to slightly tweak and fine tune the flow of energy. Finally, the unbelievable truth!

"Yeah!" Elijah shouted. He realized the room is filled with O2 (diatomic oxygen atoms). A barrage of oxygen molecules melded together, appearing spherical in a pinkish red thickened skin with a holographic appearance. All of the anomalies began to appear one by one in its harmonious true state.

Through this exhilarating experience, Elijah felt inundated with God's presence. His heart was overjoyed and thumped with excitement. He reached out and swept his hand in appreciation of the now seen reality of patterns. Thinking of sharing this moment with his father, he muttered a humble prayer and felt his presence.

Spectra

Overwhelmed in seeing what no one had ever seen before, Elijah then set his sights on the enormous outer spherical field of energy called Spectra. Spectra was the all of all, the complete timeless reality of the Universe from the beginning to its end. Spectra was absorbing, recording, and deciphering every cell, atom or molecule, every grain of sand, stone or planet, every living thing, past present and future, every second of every moment logged and accessible.

Elijah felt it may be connected directly to the Creator through another bio-electric frequency. Elijah geared up and collected the vital equipment he was going to take on a vessel, to the central part of the Universe. He traveled swiftly and within hours was passing through numerous wormholes. He planned to investigate the records and makeup of this tremendous anomaly.

He finally arrived in the vicinity of the Spectra field and quickly set up his equipment. Connecting a new mobile view sensor, which was compatible to the Convex Glasses and mounted on the outside of the vessel, he focused in on the outer spherical field skin of Spectra. He saw hubs of dimples in the trillions along with webbed frequencies, bright and white with a tint of blue, shooting out in every direction, but magnetically clustered.

 Elijah took a closer look and discerned that all the dimples of the hubs were the carved birthplaces of all the spirit energies since the beginning of creation. He was pleased to see many of the spirit energies in this vibrant state but realized that only a few have reached the purification status. Elijah stared and wondered if his father had reached this state, given the fact that he was a special person.

"Where does is it go from here?" Elijah asked himself as he tinkered with the equipment, making the necessary adjustments while trying to figure out where the frequencies are headed. The readings were coming back to him and he took off to track the frequency emanating from Spectra. He accelerated his vessel, warping into one wormhole after another, to eventually reach the barrier reef *(outer sphere)* of the Universe.

Until this point, no one was unable to decipher the Universe's outer skin because no one can tell where it begins or ends. Elijah's inventions had given the exact location, but it was impossible to travel past this point. Not only did the Universe halt there, but it was a dimensionless void.

Elijah reached a place where he felt the Creator's presence even though it is afar. Filled with fear and awe, Elijah watched through the ship's mobile convex lenses, but he only saw the lonely lighted frequency extend to an immeasurable distance.

 Elijah asked himself, "Do I have the permission or right to do this quest of connecting or communicating with this heavenly force? Would it be alright for the purpose of helping others or gaining graces having come this far? For my quest is clear, to save the burgeoning populations of Earth from unnecessary suffering and provide assistance to those who seek it."

After making his final analysis, Elijah collected himself and headed for home. He made a stop on the far-side of the moon to visit some friends while his ship received maintenance. Another important part of his layover was his introduction to the new head of the Council, Aligious' successor, who was an old colleague of his father.

Elijah confided with the new head his need for support as the human race had too many conflicts amongst their religions. When he eventually told his fully developed initial plan, it was greeted with excitement as the long-awaited answer to resolving the religious conflicts on Earth. "This new idea will have the full support of the Council," says the Council leader as a secret handshake closed their discussion. Elijah returned to his ship and headed back to his laboratory at Mount Horeb.

Moldavite Crystal

Back in his laboratory, smitten with confidence, Elijah tried to search for a similar match or molecular makeup of the lighted green frequency connected to Spectra. The database results matched a *green* rock called Moldavite. The Moldavite crystal stone is of Tektite classification, a crystal stone formed by interplanetary and meteorically high impact collisions billions of years ago.

The search results likewise indicated that the rare stone can only be found near the Moldau River in a country on Earth called Czechoslovakia. Elijah's excitement grew when he learned that the stone was well noted for its ability to send and receive intense frequencies and store an endless amount of data and information.

Arriving in Czechoslovakia above the River Moldau, Elijah hovered in midair to survey the topography along the river. He was being careful because the surrounding area had a very dense population of people. Elijah did not want to draw attention because of the ethical directive. Elijah plugged in the criterion requirements into the main computer connected to the scanning equipment to select the best possible Tektite crystal rock that would meet his specifications.

At this time, Elijah was high in the sky bordering the stratosphere and out of sight, waiting patiently. A sudden blurb noise came from the equipment, indicating a positive match. A quick smile appeared on Elijah's face as he flashed a beam of light upon the designated location. The stone rolled easily into the magnetized field beam and was consequently stored in the compartment holding area.

Back at Mount Horeb, Elijah placed the Tektite Crystal Stone carefully on a dolly-cart, wrapped it in a protective blanket, and transported it to his laboratory. After cleaning the stone and placing it in a floating harness stand to be scanned and studied, he became quite curious why the computer had chosen this rock above all.

The stone measured 2.9 feet across with a smooth oval shape. Elijah moved his hand against the surface of the crystal, studying the geometrical shape formations of its different facets. He studied its patterns and spatial dimensions to determine the specific characteristics that can possibly help it successful connect to the conduit or directly to the Force/Creator.

Diagnostics were run on the stone in all categories to decide what part of the stone would be appropriate for downloading the data. Elijah transferred the scanned data to the main computer and began to siphon many terabits of data into a part of the crystal. Amazingly, all of this information and command programming was absorbed by only a *minute* portion of the stone.

The next step would have to be done in space. Before traveling, Elijah contacted a great friend of his. Peter was a colleague during Elijah's internship on the Moon, as well as a neighbor in Adelaide. Other than his father, Peter was the only one to call him Eli. They worked well with each other in the past and Peter was excited to be working with Elijah again.

Together, they chose the furthest orbital zone from Earth so as not to encounter space debris and space devices in the closer orbits. As they prepared for the stone's release into space, Peter asked, "Eli, since the frequency we are about to power up is tiny in comparison to the main tubular frequency, isn't it questionable to send it into a realm where the eminence of the Creator is or part of?"

"Do not worry, God is in everything!" Elijah responded with a nervous grin.

As they unloaded the crystal, it seemed surreal amongst the stillness of space. The rock appeared to float stagnant until Elijah struck the key, sending a miniature tubular signal to the barrier reef (end of the Universe). While Peter watched the monitor, Elijah sent a signal that ignited all of the functions of the stone including real time delivery of data, and transmission and reception of responses.

Looking at each other without a sound, Elijah put on his Convex Specs while Peter turned on the Convex outer ship lenses. The two displays were linked to the monitors so both of them can view the inter-dimensional frequencies. Peter motioned thumbs up and engaged the light green translucent micro-frequency past the barrier towards the Creator's Force.

The light green frequency flowed instantly to the barrier reef and suddenly data streamed unto the monitors, quick and precise. Both men were stunned, as they stared at each other in silence. There was a sudden burst of happiness between them as they looked at the incoming data.

Peter and Elijah carefully approached the monitors and read the detailed results. Tears of joy filled both men as the information they received went beyond their original scope of work. After they settled from their excitement, they put in additional command questions from over a thousand different languages to communicate.

They posed the question "How are you?" They waited and looked for a response, even retrying a second and third time, but there was no response. To successfully communicate was extremely satisfying even if they got a "no" response.

Elijah did feel the energy at hand and believed there must be a *Chosen Purpose* why something sacred happened to them. Peter called it "The Holy Spirit," represented by a white dove, because Elijah poetically described the soft bright energy, "As feathers from a Dove, its sails Mercy & Love."

CHAPTER ELEVEN

ARTICLES OF FAITH

The information had been uploaded into the Moldavite Crystal and Elijah was hopeful the answers he will receive will result in the best probable outcome for saving the humans on Earth.

Elijah patiently waited for the finished response from the Creator's energy. He was hoping to advance the human race, much like his father, by teaching and witnessing what they need to reach the civilized natural requirement of the Council. He wanted humans to qualify to interact amongst the Union of Planets.

Elijah and Peter were jittery with excitement, yet extremely reverent, of the sacredness that will be revealed to them. Gathering their thoughts, they began mapping the data on the largest screen. They stood shoulder to shoulder, their body language subtle and inadvertently mirroring each other. Both of them waited attentively with nervous energy until the end data was ready for analysis. They eagerly read the first portion.

The initial results exceeded their expectations. The precision and depth of the response startled them both. They began to understand why the data was so straightforward and they embraced the results.

One of the results confirmed an intuition Elijah had regarding when to commence his important work. The seeding commencement should take place two thousand seventeen years in the distant past to have the best possible effect. Elijah and Peter decided to call this list of informational data results the "Articles of Faith." They were mystified by the list because it seemed abbreviated, yet to the point. It would be the first time that the Creator would be referred to as the "Holy Trinity" meaning and connecting the "Father, Son and Holy Spirit."

The Council reviewed the Articles of Faith and approved them with certitude for immediate execution. Elijah and Peter recruited a carefully selected few to join them in the delicate task of carrying out the Articles of Faith successfully. A docket outline of tasks began with the placement of the Moldavite Stone in the correct time zone at the exact location. The time and place were chosen. With the assistance of the Meta Mechin temporal placement device, it was moved to a time approximately two thousand years earlier.

The secrets of the Universe were within reach.

Chapter Twelve

The Birth Choice

The preparation was on. Elijah sent Gabriel, well regarded as the most majestic confrere amongst the elite and his most talented and intellectual colleague, to deliver a very important message.

The first step, according to the Articles of Faith's best probable result, should be an annunciation (announcement) to a young girl named Mary, daughter of Anne and Joachim of Nazareth in Galilee. The young maiden was to be told that she would become the maternal incarnate of a child through the Feathered Spirit of the Creator. The child's name would translate to "God Saves," and he would be called Yeshua.

When Gabriel appeared to Mary and announced the good news, her complete and immediate acceptance was a perfect response in virtue and humility. She said, "The Lord's word, unto us accordingly, it shall be done."

A few months prior, another woman was with child. She was Mary's great cousin Elizabeth, who was from the bloodline of the daughters of Aaron, brother and spokesman of the prophet Moses. The conception and birth from the two women would take place at separate times, but within a few months of each other.

The first child from Elizabeth would follow the DNA script of a Centurion (pure human DNA) so he would have the characteristics and healing abilities like that of Elijah's. Elijah followed the instructions in sequencing strands of his own DNA while including the physical traits of the soon to be parents. This special offspring would become the preacher of all religions and would be called John.

For the conception of the second child, "The Redeemer," the natural "pure" portion of Centurion DNA would be joined with the Feathered

Spirit Energy of the Creator. The physical attributes of the human DNA would come from the parents.

The conception began with the room bathed in a soft reflective light as the Creator's Spirit was at hand. The Spirit's frequency resulted in a residual biological signature directed towards Mary. The pure biological signature of informational light and sound passed peacefully through her left ear, sprinkled her temporal lobe with vibratory lighted particles, and filled her being as the wondrous course of sowing and transformation was upon the young maiden. Mary was completely in a glorious state and accepted the miracle to be one with the Spirit of the Creator.

Gabriel told Mary, "The Lord is with thee and you are now Full of Grace, blessed are you among women." Mary smiled with radiance, filled with the Creator's presence, and joy flooded Gabriel's heart, a moment he would cherish forever.

Gabriel informed Mary before departing that her cousin Elizabeth, who was beyond childbearing age and seemingly unable to conceive, was now with child. Mary became excited and was eager to see her cousin who lived with her husband Zachariah in the hill country of Judah.

In following the Articles of Faith, Gabriel had visited Elizabeth and Zachariah previously and spoke to Elizabeth who welcomed the idea of bearing a son named John. She was elated with the idea that her son would be the one delivering the anointed messages and opening the ears of so many to the coming of the Redeemer.

Zachariah, on the other hand, resisted. Gabriel explained to him how his great ancestors persevered through great trials to save their own people. "Great men such as Abraham and his devoted wife Sarah were childless until divine intervention allowed her to bear a child, Isaac," Gabriel pointed out. "Another example would be the birth of Samson to the barren Manoah. Even Noah was of this birth and lineage and thereto of greatness."

But Zachariah was unwilling to listen, even more so when he was told that his wife had been barren all this time, not because of her, but because of him. With no chance for an amicable resolution, Zachariah was rendered mute and unable to speak for a period of time so the success of the plan to save so many would not be hindered.

Unlike Zachariah, Yosef, who was betrothed to Mary (the beginning stage of a Jewish marriage), accepted wholeheartedly the gift of the Savior after an angel appeared in his dream. He was told not to fear and to feel confident making Mary his virgin wife.

Yosef was a carpenter from Nazareth whose genealogy stemmed from the tribe of Judah, connected with the House of David. Months later, he found himself back in his hometown of Bethlehem with his wife Mary to register in the Census of Quirinius. This was a decree sent out by the Roman Emperor Augustus in order to collect taxes.

Yosef and Mary could not find any lodging and found themselves desperately in search of a place to stay. Both felt that the baby was at hand, but they met resistance wherever they went. The Articles of Faith stated that an impoverish setting was imperative for the child's birth to weed out materialistic and judgmental ignorance.

Steered to a bare dwelling used for storage, the carpenter Yosef immediately scrambled to utilize pieces of angled wood to make a manger-like crib, adding grass for softness. Frantic and worried, Yosef began pacing the room until he keeled over in deep slumber.

A glow of soft pink light appeared and began curving around Mary, creating a solemn weightlessness to her being. Streaks of pink waves and blue lights enveloped the area and Mary felt a breeze, followed by a sensation of motion under her bosom. She immediately lifted up her arms to a caress of peaceful tranquility and embraced her newborn Child, whose big eyes are as bright as a star.

Mary called Yosef who was startled and overjoyed upon beholding his cherished Son. She lifted up the Baby wrapped in swaddling linen made from soft flax that she had spun herself. (This linen would be given the namesake, "Reverence Cloth," in the future.) All through the night,

Elijah, Peter, and Gabriel monitored the entire area high above in a vessel, shining like a beacon of eastern light.

Elijah's gleaming ship was positioned directly over the dwelling where the Savior slept silently. Three men appeared from the light and they were Elijah, Peter, and Gabriel. They were eager to meet the Baby and entered with gifts in their hands. One was gold for the journey the new family would undertake to Egypt, another was frankincense for use as a special healing agent and the last one was myrrh for protection against any disease.

The townspeople observed this group of sharp and distinguished foreign men (kings from distant lands) visiting the area and celebrated the birth of the Savior in the place referred to as the "Nativity." These foreign Kings from the East would then become known as the Magi.

"The more in reality you are, the closer you are to salvation." - Elijah, the secret prospective.

Immediately after Yeshua's birth, a flurry of information appeared on the Articles of Faith, configuring segments of probable outcomes after the "Birth." Simultaneously, the Moldavite Stone in space lost transmission with the main intelligence system.

Gabriel and Peter were about to leave to investigate when suddenly Elijah screamed out, "Wait!" They went back to the room to see Elijah disoriented and flushed. Before they could ask any questions, Elijah explained, "This is incomprehensible! It is stated that our Savior/Redeemer will endure a brutal scourging and be subject to great suffering, and then he will be crucified…"

Elijah was barely able to complete the sentence as the word DEATH came out from his lips. Gabriel grabbed onto Elijah as his knees collapsed to the ground. Peter looked intently at the monitor to figure out if anything can be done.

Elijah was feeling an overwhelming amount of guilt even though he understood that it was for the betterment of mankind. Eventually, Yeshua Himself will comfort Elijah for what he was feeling. In their moments together, Elijah would bond with Yeshua and cherish them with devotion the same way Aligious was devoted to Elijah.

Thinking that something might be wrong, the men traveled quickly outside the atmosphere to check on the Stone's whereabouts. Astonished to learn that the Stone was missing, they tracked its trajectory fall from orbit, landing on Earth in a fiery sphere of speed.

The Stone was the liaison between Yeshua and the Creator's Spirit source but now the connection was severed. They heaved a great sigh of relief when the data confirmed that the invisible light frequency of the Creator was now in direct connectivity with the Infant Savior, sans the assistance of the Moldavite Gem.

The Articles of Faith stated that the Moldavite Crystal Stone had to be retrieved and brought back in time to various periods. Going back to Abraham's time, Elijah had to explain to Abraham and his son Ishmael about the importance of the Stone. He gave an accurate description of the sacred Stone, stating that Yahweh/Allah/Jehovah/Mary and God's Spirit flowed through the rock and remained in this relic.

The Stone was temporarily stored at Tabor Mountain in Nazareth where there was a mountain base facility enclosed in a cave. It was where Elijah, Peter and Gabriel lived while keeping watch over Yeshua and monitoring events since He was born.

The Stone itself had taken on a different appearance due to its entry into Earth's atmosphere from space. Because it had endured a high amount of burning heat, it changed the outermost part of the Stone from a brilliant green to a brownish black film coat. It was given to a few, select prophets who would try to lead the human race and unite them as one.

In 605 AD, the last prophet sent by the Heavens of the Creative Spirit was given possession of the Moldavite Stone. Mohammed, whose name means "Praiseworthy," placed the Crystal Stone along with the "Cloth of Reverence" into its sacred area where it peacefully reposed. It is now revered as the "Hajar al Aswad," "The Black Stone" at the Kaaba in the Holy City of Mecca.

CHAPTER THIRTEEN

MENTOR

Elijah established a guardian/foster role with the young Child and made efforts to ensure Yeshua would have a fun-filled childhood with Yosef and Mary.

Any given day as a toddler, Yeshua would play in a matted area, arranging wooden figurines that Yosef had carved for Him. He offered a smile to anyone who passed by. His rosy cheeks were polished by His thick golden curls while the brilliance of the sun brightened His blue azure eyes.

When Yeshua was slightly older, Yosef designed for him a little wooden carrier to hold miniature handheld devices such as saws, chisels, and other carving and carpentry tools. He taught the boy numerous mechanical techniques for assembling structural woodwork, and together they built little carts, sailboats, and animal figurines.

Yosef was always patient and considerate to his family. Although he was the head of the household, he never acted in a supreme manner, keeping a consistent harmonious hum in their lives.

There were many glorious days of Yeshua playing with His friends and spending time with His family. One particular day Yeshua was playing in the field, His slightly older cousin gave Him a little toy baby lamb (an innocent precious moment between children). The lamb had soft wool of the purest white with marbled chalcedonic eyes. Yeshua cherished the lamb and called him Sheleg (snow). The memory of hugging the soft animal remained forever in His heart.

"Knowing time has its limits is sad… no matter how long time can be." - Elijah

Yeshua watched His mother tend to the fig trees at their vegetable garden, with plots of daisies and other colorful flowers beautifying the area around their home. From time to time, Yeshua would bloom all the different flowers at the same time so His mother could enjoy a florid display of efflorescence regardless of the season. Yeshua savored these moments with special gratitude and thankful prayers to God his Father for granting Him such a loving household.

At the age of twelve, Yeshua and His parents traveled for the Festival of the Passover to Jerusalem. After the festival was finished, they went back home with a caravan of pilgrims. But when Yosef and Mary reached their house, they realized that Yeshua was not with the group like they assumed. They concluded He was missing and were filled with an overwhelming feeling of anxiety. They immediately set out for Jerusalem to search for Yeshua.

Meanwhile, Yeshua remained in Jerusalem, studying the scriptures in the temple. He was also discussing them with the rabbis and the scholars. One of the scholars was intrigued by Yeshua's advanced intellect. He brought Yeshua to a room filled with men and announced that Yeshua of Nazareth will do the next scripture reading.

Yeshua approached the wooden pulpit, knowing the scholar's intent. Soft voices murmured how young the Child appeared. Yeshua was unshaken and took the scroll from an elder with a small bow and a meek smile, then put it down on the center of the angled reading platform. He spread apart the ancient scroll gingerly and began to read.

The whispering in the audience disappeared as Yeshua read the Torah without hesitating or missing a single word. His elders became silent and mesmerized by the fluency of the young Boy. Not once did He look back down at the long length scripture while He was reading. He fluently recited the entire scripture as if from memory.

Afterwards, whispers were heard asking, "How can this be?" A few of the scholars approached Yeshua as He was about to leave the room. Several priests were discussing His amazing reading abilities amongst themselves, trying to make sense of it. They wanted to know how He came to have such great speaking abilities and a deep grasp of the scriptures.

Three days passed before Yosef and Mary reached Jerusalem to find Yeshua near the outside entrance of the temple, talking to some scholars who were undoubtedly impressed with His words. Yeshua informed the gentlemen that He had to depart as He saw His parents approaching.

His mother was distraught and said, "Your father and I have been pining and searching for You, all of three days! Yeshua, why would You give us this anxiety?"

Yeshua responded with great concern. "You do not have to search for Me for I am in My Father's house doing His work." Mary tried her best to understand but her tears still fell as she was emotionally knotted for three days. Even though Yeshua respected His parents, this moment was necessary so they will be ready for what is to come.

The years passed and many duties were accomplished that were required by the Articles of Faith. Later in his youth, Yeshua would travel to two different Erudition Facilities for learning. One of these places was an underground city located between Cairo and Alexandria in Egypt, and the other was under the Hercules Dome in Antarctica reminiscent of the school Elijah and the other prophets went to. It was necessary for Yeshua's development to help Him prepare for His ministry. For the first time, one Man was allowed to visit the territories of all the Factions.

Yeshua possessed the ability to understand the problems of all cultures. In His travels, He demonstrated an amazing ability to speak every language of those He came into contact with. In addition, He was well versed in the particular dialect (vernacular) of the town he was visiting. This allowed him to communicate with the inhabitants on a much deeper level. Peter and Elijah concluded that since Yeshua's birth, he not only absorbed the complete knowledge of Earth's database, but also entire sectors' informational archives.

Elijah, Peter, and Gabriel took Yeshua to different strategic time periods and locations around the globe. It was during His younger years that they took Him to Egypt, Greece, India, Tibet, Britain, North America, South America, and many more. His travels included time periods as far back as thousands of years and some closer to the present days.

Yosef's physical health was, in the meantime, declining and Yeshua accompanied and helped His father as he prepared for death. Yosef chose a soft bed near his carpentry workroom as his final resting place. He wanted to spare his wife from associating common areas of their house to his death and affecting her.

Being around his tools and shop gave Yosef great comfort. In the middle of the roof, Yosef designed small openings for the sun to peek through. On this summer day, several lighted rays seemed to be angled at the head of Yosef's bed, illuminating his face.

Yosef's breaths were becoming shorter each time he attempted to speak. He spotted a sparrow on a bucket, sipping water and singing, which made him smile. Yeshua took His father's hand and brought it close to His chest near His heart. Yeshua began to pray in a very personal way and raised His father's hand to His lips so He may kiss it.

Yeshua then put down his father's hand to rest gently on his chest and heard the silent sobs of His mother, pacing in the adjacent room. She heard the beautiful blessings of her Son to His father. She witnessed how the fearful, bitter part of death can be removed.

Yeshua's pure love flowed as Yosef's soul prepared for the transition to Heaven. The old man began to lose color and appeared dull and pale as he gasped his last few breaths. Mary hurried over with a slurred, "No," under her breath and knelt at the side of the bed. Yeshua reached out to comfort His mother.

Suddenly, the birds outside became silent and still. Yosef's eyes became lifeless with a final stare at the faces of his beloved Son and wife. Mary's head fell on Yeshua's shoulder as she let out an uncontrollable cry. She was overwhelmed with grief and found comfort in the embrace of her Son, knowing that one day He will share His everlasting Life.

In the days that followed, Yeshua took control of His father's carpentry shop and clients. He set up a fair system so the remaining workers can continue to make a living while providing a steady income to Mary's household. He had a great relationship with His father's employees, and they gave Mary and Yeshua reassurance that the status quo would be maintained. Most importantly, the men would provide for and protect His mother when Yeshua began traveling and spending long periods of time away from home.

Dead Sea Scrolls

Approaching thirty years of extraordinary achievements at the highest level, Yeshua was still preparing for His ultimate ministry. His works were being overseen by Elijah and his colleagues, in accordance with the Articles of Faith.

Elijah decided to bring Yeshua to the 20th century during the 1940's. The location was Israel's Judean Desert, approximately one and a half kilometers inland from the Dead Sea's northwest shore at Khirbet Qumran in the West Bank. They brought with them scrolls of one thousand texts from the Essenes' archives dating back to the second century before Christ's time. But added to this collection was the last of the scrolls, the twelfth scroll. The golden scroll contained the events and interactions in Elijah's life (Book of Elijah), culminating to the Savior's (Yeshua) Second Coming.

The Essenes were special members of a monastic brotherhood in Palestine who oversaw the unique events and various interpretations pertaining to the lineage of the Holy Families since the time of their creation. Elijah and Yeshua chose excerpts from an assortment of antiquity writings in the Hebrew Testament (Bible, Book of Genesis) and in the Essenes' scrolls, setting them together in a bounded book.

While breaking bread and sharing wine, they divided more voluminous number of additional texts into twelve parts (scrolls) and placed them in twelve distinctive caves throughout the cliffs of Khirbet Qumran. Elijah encouraged Yeshua to include an additional 30 texts about His early life. "These 30 texts consist of one text for every year of Your life, yet additional texts will be appended," Elijah said. "The first to the final text will explain the Immaculate Conception of Mary all the way through to the New Beginning of Your life. It will also include the family ancestry and genealogy connection to directly link the Old Testament with the New Testament."

All the caves were filled with the documents except for the 12th and last cave. Yeshua walked slowly to it, supporting the documents in His bent arms, until He disappeared into the shadows of the cave. He carried what will be the keystone of all scriptures which is the "Golden Scroll (Book of Elijah)."

Yeshua reappeared, His eyes looking like two sapphires reflecting the feathered light. They discussed how the Scrolls will be found and arranged that it will be by a young man, only a few years ahead of this time (1940's).

They returned to Yeshua's time period by the Sea of Galilee to choose His disciples. He gathered unusually plain and ordinary non-scholars to follow Him. Some were fishermen, one is a tax collector, and another was a former revolutionist.

All of the men shared one important commonality as future disciples. They all had above average levels of Centurion DNA in their genomes and two of them were pure Centurion, much like John the Baptist. These genomes (a dozen dormant strands) can be activated at a later time to possess the ability to heal the sick and perform miracles.

Yeshua gathered the twelve apostles, representing and emulating the twelve Hebrew Tribes. The tribes originated from the twelve Factions that were assigned to Earth, signaling the movement of teachings to accelerate the growth of all people on Earth.

Yeshua felt compelled to change some of the names of the disciples so they can represent highly regarded men who devoted their lives to selflessness and love. Most importantly, He chose Simon to follow Him and changed his name to Peter to honor one of His mentors and good friends.

Transfiguration

Traveling back to Nazareth, Yeshua and the twelve disciples arrived at His childhood residence to introduce His mother Mary to the twelve chosen men who will be doing God's work. Yeshua asked His mother to accommodate nine of the disciples while Peter, James and John went with Him to Mount Tabor. Upon His return, they would celebrate His milestone birthday and the beginning of His Ministry.

Yeshua set out for the mountain with the three disciples. He felt a tingling right above His head and knew that the Nimbus Metamorphosis is about to engage because He had reached the right age. He was about to possess the halo of energy that was customarily bestowed upon the bloodlines of His heritage.

Midway up the mountain, Yeshua told his disciples to rest so they could witness and understand the transformation (The Transfiguration) about to take place. By witnessing the event, it would give them all the graces they need to do the Father's (Creator's) Work (Articles of Faith).

Looking up, Peter, James and John saw a cloud forming at the top of the mountain and heard a pulsating hum, followed by an accumulation of vapors below the cloud. Hidden within the cloud, they saw a large shield of great brightness. Yeshua walked up the mountain towards the cloud, when two figures started to descend side by side to Yeshua. One was on His right and the other was on His left, seven feet above the ground. Two beams of concentrated light bound the two men, with Elijah to the right of Yeshua and Moses to the left. The disciple Peter was astonished at what he saw while John and James smiled.

During the Transfiguration of Yeshua, a spiritual illuminated energy of glorified joy was exchanged. It circulated and appeared like lighted wings half-opened. Yeshua appeared ready to fly up to the heavens as a feathery soft brightness floated above His head.

Elijah and Moses ascended back up to the cloud, leaving Peter in a transfixed state of mind as he wondered what had just happened. Suddenly, a voice from within the cloud said, "He is the Chosen Son of Man, listen to Him." Then, in a blink of an eye, everything evaporated and disappeared.

All was normal once again when they returned to Mary's house. Peter, James, and John were instructed not to mention what they had just witnessed, for now. It was only for them to know at this time, but to be revealed once the Son of Man rose from the dead. The disciples vaguely understood and did not challenge or ask why. They obediently made their way back to the celebration.

Before Yeshua's ministry began, there was a legion of schooled evangelists and laypersons spreading the "word" throughout the land. However, there was only one evangelist who awed and drew hundreds upon hundreds of people to be baptized with water. He was the cousin of Yeshua, John.

Elijah was very close to John and treated him like a son. In addition, Elijah was his mentor along with a few colleagues who attended the Erudition School.

John was a quiet individual but when he preached the word of God, his heart became an inferno of passion, love, repentance, and forgiveness. His main objective was to herald in the Christ (Yeshua) and in doing so, he used water to cleanse and purify one's spirit. This act had people waiting in masses to be baptized. John's message was spreading throughout the southernmost part of Israel, creating fear in the leaders of the region especially King Herod (a Roman-appointed King of the Judea territory).

The day had come for John, the Baptist, to meet his cousin, the Messiah. When he saw Yeshua approaching him in the river to be baptized, John hesitated. "I am not worthy of baptizing You, oh Lord. I should be begging for You to baptize me."

Yeshua bowed His head towards John and said, "I am Yeshua whose turn amongst many has come to be baptized. Let it be done." As John baptized Yeshua, the sun left its position in the sky and descended to a soft white cloud above the crowd. There were glares everywhere from the blinding light as a voice proclaimed, "This is the Son that has been chosen for all, listen to Him."

John said to Yeshua, "I baptize You with the Holy Spirit." When John was finished, he looked up at the people and shouted, "Behold the Lamb of God." He then looked directly at Yeshua and whispered, "Who takes away the sins of the world." John spoke it quietly, direct to Yeshua, because he knew why He walked the Earth. He knew announcing it publicly would be considered blasphemy and put them both in danger.

While serving as the forerunner for the coming of the Messiah, John the Baptist was fulfilling Elijah's prophecy (Articles of Faith). Through his voice, John would be the preparer of the "Word made Flesh" and "Behold the Lamb of God." John had brought this prophesy to reality through his acts and the connection he made with Yeshua.

Soon after, John the Baptist was arrested. It was foretold that it would be the era-point that began Yeshua's ministry. After John the Baptist's arrest, King Herod decided to behead him because he feared that people who were known to carry the "Light" can be reborn and therefore threaten the (King's position) kingdom with their miraculous return.

CHAPTER FOURTEEN

DESERT

According to the Articles of Faith, once John the Baptist was arrested, the Son of Man would start His ministry. With many trials of temptation, he traveled through a barren dry desert, enduring suffering, fasting, and being put to the spiritual test by outside forces. This was a quest that many of his predecessors had successfully completed, including both Moses and Elijah.

The twisted desert area encompassed the region between Jerusalem and the Dead Sea. The desert was a maze of wadis (ravines) and mountainous terrain. It had twelve-hundred-foot mountain peaks (escarpments) that were dangerous to pass upon. It was a journey of three major allurements (temptations), "Forbidden Food, Testing God and Kingdom Reigns."

Immediately, Yeshua felt the scarcity of food and found Himself weak. It occurred after just three days even though He was in prime physical condition. It was only through His prayers and prayers alone that He was able to bring Himself to the Seventh Day.

Yeshua glanced at one of the shelters, high above the summit of the Judaean Mountain. He saw a round shaded cave, carved out of the mountain. He struggled to reach the summit because dust was being blown into His eyes, and He was using His arms and stomach to crawl up the steep slope.

Upon arriving in the cave, relief overcame Yeshua. Suddenly, a voice from within the cave said, "Look down before You!" Yeshua noticed two stones about the size of a fist, projecting an image of two loaves of freshly baked bread. The voice continued, "If You are One with God, just reach or say the word and the stones will become bread!"

Yeshua fervently recited, "Man shall not live on bread alone, but with the Spirit that comes from the Mouth of God!" A bouquet of fragrance filled the grotto and Yeshua woke up the next day, feeling nourished and rested. He set forth on the mountain ridge, seeing numerous ravines and miles of boulders.

Yeshua mapped the terrain in His mind, trying to pick the path with the least resistance between the labyrinths of stones. He chose an amicable path to follow, finding Himself stopping, going, and resting, again and again. Finally, He saw in the distance a cliff with a natural opening alongside a plateau. It was now the twelfth day and a critical point in His journey.

Yeshua climbed to a shaded cave high onto the cliff when a voice echoed from below. "You have to endure more than three times this grueling experience and vastness ahead of You. You are near the point of no return. You can still go back now." The voice continued (as written in the Psalms), "Those who put their trust in God will receive protection. So as not to endure more suffering, just throw Yourself in the air off the cliff and take flight as would a bird, for You are the Son of Man and will be saved."

Yeshua stated, "It is written to have faith and trust in God. Do not put God to the Test!" He dusted off His sandals and moved onward.

Days passed and Yeshua began his difficult downward trek. The rocks were positioned on an angled contour that became narrower as one came down. Between His fatigue and the dangerous rock formation, it would be a deadly descent.

Yeshua took a piece of cloth from His tunic and utilized part of a leather rope to tie around the sharp edge of a rock for a secure hold. He bent and lowered his body into the ravine, wedged against the rocks. He used the scarce grass for water, and it was enough to enable him to complete his thirty third day in the desert.

As Yeshua approached the final historic point, He saw multiple doorways carved into the mountain. He smiled as He spotted a natural source of water dribbling on the rocks. He clambered up the rugged mountain face and scrambled towards the water beside the doorway.

Suddenly, a field of lighted colors surrounded Yeshua and halted His approach. Bits and pieces of spherical particles spun and formed a beautiful landscape of all the Kingdoms of the world in their brilliancy. Yeshua was pictured in His glory, well-nourished and powerful. A voice emitted from the charming apparition, saying, "All that You see will become Yours, just bow by my side and idolize me with reverence!"

Yeshua quickly replied, "Worship the Lord your God and serve Him only!" Depleted, He still found the strength to say, "Away from Me!" It was the last of the great tests. Yeshua had proved to be worthy of His mission by completing and passing the Three Temptations.

Following his journey into the desert, Yeshua rested for three days. Elijah and other honored guests attended an honorary solemn ceremony in recognition of His success. Ordinary meetings were put on hold until after the ceremony.

The 40 days and 40 nights are represented in the Christian-based Lenten holiday, starting with "Ash Wednesday" which is approximately 46 days before Easter. The Ash Wednesday ceremony uses the burnt remains of blessed palms to anoint one's forehead with the sign of the cross. The ashes are from the collected palms from the previous year's Palm Sunday. Ash Wednesday is a day of fasting wherein a person sacrifices something desirable for a period of 40 days. This is the beginning of repentance and sacrifice leading up to Easter, furthering the connection between the purification of Baptism and the cleansing of the Temptation of Christ in the Desert.

CHAPTER FIFTEEN

THREE-YEAR MINISTRY

Yeshua's divine humanity felt physical and emotional pain, hunger, and even death. Nevertheless, His miracles and teachings were true evidence of His soul's divinity.

At the beginning of His ministry, Yeshua and His disciples attended a wedding in the area of Cana. This was where Yeshua performed His first miracle humbly at the request of His mother. He asked that the servants fill up to the brim the empty jugs with water, and He miraculously turned the water into wine. The significance of this miracle was compared to Moses turning water into blood and when Yeshua performed the great miracle at the Last Supper, changing the bread into His body and the wine into His blood.

It was Yeshua's last miracle before His ultimate sacrifice, The Passion of Christ. His acts of ministry were not done with fearful intimidation, but by acts of pure love and compassion for all the suffering sinners.

"Do not believe Me unless I do what my Father does. But if I do it, even though you do not believe Me, believe the miracles, that you may know and understand that the Father is in Me and I in the Father." - Yeshua

Elijah stayed close by overseeing from a distance the "Three-Year Ministry" of Yeshua. By the end of His ministry, Yeshua had covered a vast area of land, traveling by foot to various cities and towns. It included Capernaum, Gennesaret, Syrian-Phoenicia, Bethsaida, Caesarea Philippi, Trachonitis, Mt Tabor, Jerusalem, Galilee, Judea, and Samaria. Elijah identified these regions as the "Promise Land."

During those travels, Yeshua remained humble, not using an authoritative influence while performing miracles that were divinely inspired. They would include but were not limited to curing and healing the lepers, paralytics, blind, deaf, dumb, and possessed as well as raising the dead. As a result, Yeshua's popularity grew to a point that a few religious leaders felt He was a threat to their powerful positions among the people. They could not accept that a humble carpenter from Nazareth would be the Messiah and attempted to seize His power and remove Him of His entirety.

There were many times that Elijah and Yeshua would communicate over the three-year period. However, only one major public appearance occurred. This was during the Transfiguration with Yeshua's disciples present. All through the Three-Year Ministry, Yeshua touched upon the sacred interests of the Articles of Faith.

Studies have proven that wine and water can sustain memory. As priests perform this ritual, they actually bend their head towards the wine and speak directly into the chalice that is holding the water and wine, proclaiming the words and signifying Yeshua's connection with God represented in the Last Supper.

CHAPTER SIXTEEN

THE PASSION

Passion can have two meanings. It can be translated as an ardent affection of love or refer to the events that led to the suffering of the Messiah, Yeshua. His death on the cross was His passion for mankind, demonstrating the quintessential application of the word.

Yeshua was devoted to all people and cherished every moment of His ministry despite knowing the Romans would torture Him to His death for it. His unwavering perfection and devotion to His teachings would serve as the impetus (movement) that would save mankind and justify His selfless sacrifice.

Yeshua's triumphant entrance into Jerusalem, as well as other events, was predestined and foretold by very close friends of Elijah's father, Aligious. They were Micah, Isaiah and Zachariah who served right after the time of Elijah and were given certain excerpts from "The Articles of Faith" by him. This was done so they could document an accurate account of the prophecy foretold as the truth.

The chosen few prophesied that there would be a virgin that would be with child and give birth to a son named Emmanuel in Bethlehem. Additional predictions stated, "Comes to you, the Messiah, riding on a donkey, on a colt, the foal of a donkey; They will have scourged Him, then pierce His hands and feet; They divide His garments among them and cast lots for His clothing." Yeshua's purpose was clear and precise, there would be a connection from the "Book of Genesis" (Old Testament) to the New Testament.

Passover

It was an annual ritual for the Jewish people to travel to Jerusalem and gather together to commemorate the Hebrews' liberation from slavery in Egypt. They also celebrated the Passover meal with friends and family. The great Exodus led by Moses was likewise observed through the arduous (grueling) trek that Yeshua and His family took once a year during His younger days.

On this particular morning at the house of Lazarus, Yeshua was about to fulfill a prophecy. He gave instructions to a few of His disciples to acquire a donkey from a particular man (Gabriel) to ride into Jerusalem. He was precise in His directions.

According to the symbolic references of Eastern tradition, a donkey is an animal of peace which is the opposite of a horse, an animal of war. It was relevant to the Articles of Faith proclaiming He will come as the Prince of Peace, meek and sitting graciously on a donkey.

The disciples found out that Elijah had a special donkey set aside for them to bring to Yeshua. It was Gabriel who will deliver the chosen donkey, especially donated by one of the Faction council members. This donkey did not scamper and had a smooth gait, so the rider won't bounce. In addition, the donkey gave the council clear audio and visual access from afar.

Beginning His journey in late March (early spring), Yeshua descended from the Mount of Olives and prepared to enter the holy city. The nuances of nature were in bloom and many of His followers crowded Him fervently for the trip. Part of the reason for the adoring masses of bystanders was His miraculous resurrection of a man called Lazarus.

Not only did Yeshua raise Lazarus from the dead, but He also accomplished the miracle three days after the man's death. It was unheard of to bring someone back to life with decomposition already in its early stages.

His disciples felt proud to escort Yeshua and remained close to His side. It was early morning when they entered the city. Yeshua reminded His disciples not to yearn for proud positioning but rather to serve others and remember that the Son of Man will give His life as a ransom for many. The disciples' attention was alive, but the lesson on selflessness fell on deaf ears.

Yeshua saw a fig tree en route and approached it, only to see it was all leaves with no fruit. He grazed with His index finger one of the leaves and said, "May you never bear fruit again!" The tree immediately withered.

The disciples witnessed it and were perplexed as to why Yeshua would say it considering figs were not in season. "How did the fig tree wither so quickly?" they asked.

Yeshua responded, "Truly I tell you, if you have faith and no doubt, not only can you do what was done to the fig tree, but you can say to the mountain, Go, throw yourself into the sea and it will be done. If you believe, you will receive whatever you ask for in prayer."

The apostles enjoyed the happy atmosphere inside Jerusalem as the citizens waved palms in the air in a celebratory fashion. They placed their cloaks and garments on the ground to mark the path that Yeshua's animal would walk on.

The triumphant entrance into the city was fit for a King, but not the type of King the people would understand. This commemorative passage would eventually become Palm Sunday, the beginning of Holy Week which is observed by over one billion people.

Yeshua scanned the lands around Him and saw people pouring into Jerusalem. His thoughts were troubled, having knowledge of all the suffering and turmoil in the future, in the lands of Israel. He contemplated the hundreds of thousands of Jewish people who will perish violently by force and was unsettled by the sheer numbers. His body quivered as His eyes filled with tears.

Yeshua wept, knowing His Father/Creator designed the concept of time so the sins from the past can be forgiven. He was saddened, remembering that only one out of twelve people will be saved in His second coming. His heart was heavy, recalling the immense cleansing efforts of the Faction in the past and what He had to endure so it will not be in vain.

The number of people that Yeshua would enlighten and save was staggering. The Articles of Faith had chosen this region as the best probable origin for seeding the world with the Good News. The people will endure unfortunate future events and become refugees, spreading to new lands around the globe to share the Good News.

Yeshua felt deflated as He entered the temple, mostly because of the Jewish priests' presence everywhere. They had been trying to harass Yeshua and waiting for Him to commit a mistake. The chief priests needed an excuse to arrest Him because He was a threat to their comfortable, well-off positions in the Jewish community. Many attempts had been made by the chief priests to trap Him with His own words, trying to uncoil His intellect. They were always frustrated and disappointed when He gave a perfect answer to all their vexing questions. At the same time, He exposed their own weaknesses.

Yeshua's study with Elijah and His colleagues, along with His Connection to the Light, gave Yeshua a real advantage. He already knew beforehand what was going to transpire, what question would be asked. He always had the best response based on equated probability.

Once, a chief priest approached Yeshua from the crowd, offering praise and compliments to His devotion to the truth. However, his true intention was to entrap Yeshua. In a plot discussed between the high and chief priests, they anticipated that Yeshua would be opposed to taxes.

The governor at the time was Pontius Pilate, who was in charge of the Roman province of Judaea from AD 26–36. He was serving Tiberius, Emperor of Rome, and was responsible for collecting the taxes in Roman Judea with the authority to put anyone to death.

After the flattery and compliments, the chief priest asked Yeshua whether it is right for Jewish people to pay the taxes mandated by Rome. Yeshua remained silent while the chief priest provocatively spun a coin in his right hand. "Well, should we pay, or shouldn't we?" the chief priest pressed for an answer.

Yeshua asked him to produce a Roman coin that was suitable for paying taxes. The chief priest nervously handed Him the coin and He raised it for everyone to see. "Whose name and picture are on this coin?" He asked the crowd.

"Caesar's!" the crowd responded.

So Yeshua said, "Render therefore unto Caesar the things which are Caesar's and unto God the things that are God's."

But what irked the high priest most was when Yeshua saw the merchant bazaar in the temple. The courtyard was filled with livestock and the tables of money changers who exchanged one standard of currency to another for profit. It was an unfair practice, but it was the only way to purchase a pure/blessed/certified animal for sacrifice during Passover.

Greek and Roman currency, Jewish and Tyrian money were exchanged throughout. Yeshua was enraged and began overthrowing the tables of the money changers and releasing the doves from their cages. He used the woven leather rope surrounding His garment to steer the herds of livestock out of the temple.

While the people stood shocked and immobile, Yeshua proclaimed, "It is written, our Father's house shall be called the house of prayer; but you have made it a den of thieves."

Several of the chief priests witnessed the scene and quickly went to Joseph Caiaphas, the Jewish high priest, to inform him. Caiaphas had been waiting for an excuse to organize a plot to be rid of Yeshua and was inspired by the occurrence.

On "All Fools' Day," Judas Iscariot, one of the twelve original disciples of Yeshua, went to the chief of the Sanhedrin, the supreme council or tribunal of the region. Caiaphas had religious and criminal jurisdiction in the Sanhedrin council, and wanted to arrest Yeshua. It would be Judas' discussion with the council that will set the stage for entrapping Yeshua for violations against Jewish doctrine.

Judas was in charge of the disciples' monetary affairs. He took out the moneybag to be filled by the priest as payoff. Judas gave a time and location where Yeshua can be arrested and questioned by the

Sanhedrin. He set the sequence of events that will lead to the Crucifixion and Resurrection, key components from the Articles of Faith that will spur salvation for mankind.

John, the apostle, also had an important role which was why he was at every important event in the ministry of Yeshua. He was a major figure that would bring everything together. He was also one of the few disciples (the brothers James & John) that were aware of the Articles of Faith and would use the information to keep a perspective on the events to come.

Garden

The Wednesday right before his arrest, Yeshua and the apostles John and James traveled to the summit of the Mount of Olives, leaving the other apostles in Bethany. Their journey brought them to a place where they can join Elijah and his colleagues and be escorted to a historic meeting known as the Alacritous-Tribulation (Preparation for the Passion of Christ).

They arrived in the City of Adelaide, where Elijah spent most of his childhood. The group went to the Aitho Circle Building, where Elijah's father Aligious once held the highest position amongst the heads.

The Council began convening with not only the heads of each of the Factions present, but also hundreds of the most important and influential people/species of the Union of Planets in attendance. The Council explained clearly to Yeshua, John, James, Elijah, and his colleagues that they were under no obligation to go forward with the excruciating woe that had yet to happen.

All those present recognized and gave gratitude to the three honored guests who were willing to undergo the task, unparalleled in courage and selflessness. Yeshua, John and James were met with applause by the entire council. After all of the twelve members spoke, the meeting ended, and the crowd left with sincere hope and thanks.

Yeshua, John and James walked with Elijah to a hall called THW, an acronym for Temporal Historic Watchmen. This "Order" protected the time continuum from unauthorized time travel to safeguard current existence. In addition, the THW had programs that cross-reference probable outcomes. Knowing the Watchmen already had an established timeline, John and James asked the obvious, "If we follow the 'Articles of Faith,' what would be the difference towards the amount of people saved?"

Access to these databases was limited to a privileged few but Elijah had authorization and motioned his hands to a display monitor that retrieved the data. He backed away from the monitor and invited everyone to see the results. It turned out there was a 12 to 1 ratio vs. 144 to 1, per person saved, as calculated for the Second Coming of Yeshua in 2037.

Note: These results were for the number of people that Yeshua will save but small in comparison to the billions of others that had lived through the last two thousand years. All who would benefit accepted His existence and were closer to getting glorified spiritually.

Everyone was overwhelmed by the dramatic results. Elijah felt solemn and inadequate, knowing the enormous suffering Yeshua will face as well as the pain ahead for John and James. Everyone else was elated but Elijah was saddened because of his personal bond with Yeshua. He had been watching and caring for Him since He was born. He had always been there to protect Him and was uneasy with the feeling of helplessness he will experience from what was to happen.

Elijah looked over to Yeshua with a guilty stare, knowing he was responsible because of his innovations. Yeshua saw His mentor's remorse and pain. He explained to Elijah without hesitation, "If just one day is a gift, think about how many more we are all given." Elijah produced a half smile, somewhat lifted, and proceeded towards Yeshua to give Him a slow embrace.

Yeshua lifted up His hand and said, "Please Pappy, not in front of the men!" Elijah started laughing and Yeshua was delighted with Elijah's joy. He knew His humor would help ease His protector's heartbreak.

By Thursday, the mystical Last Supper was being readied by the women and the disciples. It was after sunset and the twelve disciples would share in the Passover meal. The apostles would not be able to grasp the mystical events that would transpire until many days later.

After the Last Supper, Yeshua took the remaining eleven disciples to the foot of Mount of Olives. From the gathered disciples, He chose James and John, the two sons of Zebedee who was a dear colleague of Aligious and were of Centurion bloodline. They started their ascent when Yeshua turned back towards the men left and asked, "Peter, are you not coming?"

Peter quickly stood up from the huddle of men and ran to catch up to Yeshua. He followed Yeshua to His customary place of prayer, along with James and John. The location was where Yeshua would often have visitations with Elijah.

The special area was called Gethsemane, "Garden of Olives." Located east of the Kidron Valley where the path led up to the mountain that connected Jericho, the sanctuary had rows of crops and flowers and bordered with rocks and tall wilted grass.

Yeshua told the three apostles, "Be still here and stern, pray that you will not fall into temptation!" He then withdrew from the apostles and ambled on foot to a curve beyond the olive trees to meet with Elijah and Gabriel.

Yeshua gave a warm and endearing firm hug to each of His friends. Gabriel began to apply analgesic herbs to His neck and back with tender care. Yeshua looked to Elijah for an explanation.

"We thought of using these ointments to numb your skin for a full day to lessen the pain," Elijah said.

Yeshua lifted His right hand outward in front of His heart, indicating there was no need for these ointments. He then said, "I am aware the time has come, thank you for your devotion." He released the hands of both men which He held for support. Elijah and Gabriel ascended quietly into the night sky with heart-wrenching grief.

Exhausted with sorrow, Yeshua walked back to His disciples and said, "The flesh is weak, and My Spirit is here." Filled with anguish, He tried to find His favorite place to pray. He stopped by a smooth large stone with an olive tree right beside it and began to contemplate the torture, humiliation, pain, and death He was going to go through.

Yeshua's eyes filled with tears and were unable to see a thin branch stemming out horizontally from the thick olive tree. It grazed the top of His scalp, drawing blood, and He fell to His knees. Bent and leaned over, He tried to look up and verbalized His thoughts, "Father, if You are willing to take this cup from Me; yet be it not My will, but Yours to be done!"

Yeshua's prayers became stronger as He accepted what was to come (flagellation/death), knowing His sacrifice was an act of pure love in compliance with the Articles of Faith. His tears touched the roots of the tree and as a result, this special tree would be nourished until His return. It became the oldest living (Oleaceae Family) olive tree known in history, along with several other trees that were grafted from it.

Returning to His apostles, Yeshua found them sleeping and felt disappointed they did not stay alert. Looking towards Peter, He said once again, "Pray, not to fall into temptation." He was preparing His Spirit for what was to come while Peter was being conditioned for a life-changing event (the denial) that would strengthen his spirit for the work he must carry out after Yeshua's death.

Betrayal

From a distance, a mob approached the Garden of Olives led by the disciple Judas Iscariot. Among them were the Sanhedrin guards armed with weapons. They stood and waited for a signal from the officials to arrest Yeshua. They needed confirmation as to who Yeshua was.

Judas approached Yeshua and kissed Him, signaling to the guards this was the man they wanted to arrest. The head official waved his hand towards Yeshua.

As three Sanhedrin guards approached Yeshua to take hold of Him, two other guards lagged behind to make sure they wouldn't be ambushed. Rustling his way through the soldiers was the infamous servant of the Jewish high priest, Malchus. He was an especially irritating character who in the past gave the disciples a lot of trouble and was jockeying for position to confront Yeshua.

Peter was furious with Malchus' arrogance and cowardly aggression and impulsively drew his sword to protect Yeshua. The would-be victim blocked the blow with his lantern and as a result, the sword veered off to the right and sliced off a portion of his ear.

Yeshua swept His arm and hand towards Peter and adamantly said, "No! Peter, he who draws the sword shall perish by the sword." This adage was very dear to Yeshua because of its importance on judgment day after His Second Coming. The quote would determine the outcome for so many, regarding who would be chosen and who won't be.

Yeshua said to Peter, "Put away the sword into the sheath; the cup which my Father has given Me, shall I not drink it?" He placed His hand over the wounded ear of Malchus and healed it. The high priest's servant was shocked and hypnotized by His compassion.

Yeshua then said to the guards, "It is I you are seeking, as I will come willingly but these men are innocent, leave them alone." After witnessing His miraculous healing of the servant's ear, the soldiers decided they should listen to Yeshua and marched away only with Him.

Once the priests had Yeshua in their possession, they had to conjure up a reason as to why they seized Him. Caiaphas, the high priest, was influencing the others and was encouraging them to desperately seek false evidence to frame Yeshua with. They were unable to find any.

Yeshua remained silent throughout most of the proceedings until finally Caiaphas demanded that Yeshua admit whether He was the Christ (The Son of God). Yeshua responded, "You have said so. I am, and you shall see the Son of Man sitting at the Right Hand of Power, coming again from the clouds in heaven."

Caiaphas tore his robe in dramatic fashion, signifying Yeshua will be charged with blasphemy and ordering Him to be beaten. The whole time, Yeshua fixated with a physically tired stare on the Phylactery box that was worn by the priests on the front top of their heads. The small box contained an important prayer or scripture that was carried by a particular priest in order to praise God.

Yeshua went through six different types of hearings and interrogations from the Sanhedrin, Roman authorities (hierarchies) and chief priests. Caiaphas and the other priests realized the necessity to manipulate Pontius Pilate, the Roman governor of Judea. He and he alone had the final say to hopefully condemn Yeshua to death by crucifixion.

Pilate resisted the high priest after interviewing Yeshua. He found no tangible reason to condemn Him and was annoyed. But the priests skillfully manipulated the Roman governor until he capitulated with an idea to let the people decide. It was a tradition to release one prisoner during Passover as a sign of goodwill.

Acting quickly, Caiaphas told his chief priests to pay the guards assigned at the entrance of the courtyard to bar anyone supporting Yeshua from entering the area. The action would almost guarantee His crucifixion. There were three other prisoners being held for execution and Yeshua was the fourth. One of them would be set free, in accordance with the Passover tradition.

Meanwhile, it was customary to send prisoners for scourging in order to hasten their death on the cross. Not only was it excruciating torture, but it also instilled fear in the crowds, allowing the Romans to keep control over their territories. The intense punishment consisted of lashing the back of the prisoner while tied to a stake.

The Roman guards brought the shackled prisoners to the northwest side of the fort so the scene could be monitored from Pilate's palace. En route, Yeshua passed a condensed facility area made up of clusters of old, worn horse and carriage barns adjacent to the main complex. They were now the living quarters of foreign slaves and some prisoners convicted of petty crimes.

Yeshua looked over at the old huts and saw aggressive hand motions from the overcrowded openings, followed by sarcasm from the inhabitants. The slave quarters left a harsh stench, and a wretched aroma surrounded the area. Yeshua carried on and tiredly walked in metal chains.

Continuing up alongside a lengthy limestone wall, Yeshua saw a huge fortress. He stopped and stood facing a crowd of observers on the opposite side of the road, then began moving again. There were numerous horses snorting, ridden by leathery guards who gave curt, abrupt commands. It was the well-traveled route to perdition, a prelude to what awaited around the corner.

Scourge

The sunlight bared two walls that make-up a stone corner, about ten feet in height. The base of the wall was made from blocks of limestone while the rest was mortared stone. Still, there is a third knee wall to the left of the inner corner, approximately three feet in height. The small knee wall was for bystanders to stand on and have a panoramic overview of the torturous ritual.

The Romans were infamously known for this type of punishment, and not the originators (Persia, Babylon). The pillars were laid out in a triangulated pattern in a thirty foot by thirty-foot square, with one part open. Each pillar had two assigned executioners or floggers, sometimes referred to as ruffians.

Roman soldiers who were violent criminals in the past were especially handpicked for this extreme measure of brutality. Elijah and his team watched the situation with grave difficulty, camouflaged by the clouds, and made sure not to interfere with the events below for the day had come.

Yeshua walked into the sunlight and was unnerved by the scene. He saw three thick wooden pillars protruding from the ground and fixed on the closest pillar were two rusted rings bolted on the top sides of the six-foot tall, twenty-four-inch girthed cylinder of a stake. He was in shock as He lost His breath.

Yeshua's eyes looked in the direction of the weathered gray pillars, scorched and baked by the sun. The purple tint on the wooden stake's surface appeared to be petrified remains of blood and body fluid embedded into the torturing device.

To the left is a wooden table laid out broad sided to show off the display of whips spooled up neat in a circle. This table was about ten feet long and was also used to repair any of the whips if need be. The Roman ruffians took pride in their torturous flogging devices. There were different styles of whips, sporting braided leathery stems and an assorted sadistic collection of infliction tips tied to the thongs.

Coming out from the slave dwelling, the four floggers strode towards the forum accompanied by the sound of scuffling and obscenities from a crowd in a drunken stupor. Yeshua was tired from no sleep after the many Sanhedrin and Roman trials He faced. He watched the executioners approach.

The crowd simmered down upon seeing the floggers who wore cured leather across their chests, metal shoulder pads with bands of metal around their forearms and flapped metal girds to cover their loins. Beneath the protective gear were bare hairy arms and legs covered in scars, dirty with the stench of a wild beast. They were malefactors from different lands who had been condemned for horrible crimes but, because of their cruelty and their mere size, were spared so they could be used for slave labor.

Two other executioners were unable to come because of severe headaches, due to Gabriel's intervention. It was the angel's hope that with two less floggers, the remaining executioners would pick up the slack and get tired quickly to inflict extra punishment on Yeshua.

It was a Rabbinic or Jewish law to receive a maximum of 40* lashes minus 1, for a total of 39. It was adopted by the Jewish people for a more civilized approach to the barbarism. This idea came as a representation of Moses returning from Mount Horeb after 40 days with the Ten Commandments.

*The number forty has been used repeatedly in different ancient religions. The importance of 40 is the root of the number. Plainly put, 40 as a positive integer is the sum of the first four pentagonal numbers;

it is a pentagonal pyramidal number and also an octagonal number (composite number). Sequential numbers 1, 3, 9, 27 = 40 are oddly enough how human DNA is coded with a connecting pentagonal spiral of a double helix, which connects directly to the number 40! These are the reasons why the number forty is a part of human customs and traditions.

Barabbas, who was arrested for killing a Roman soldier, was about to undergo what the executioners called a "half death" when it was his turn to be scourged. A half death was a state in which the floggers leave their victims with torn flesh and muscles, accentuated by excessive bleeding, as if the prisoners were half dead and ready for crucifixion.

Laughing, two legionnaires threw Barabbas against the pillar in front while joking about his petite, skinny body. One of the floggers named Brutus selected his whip, then looked over at the "counter caster" confirming he was ready to start. This counter caster clerk or number counter, employed by the Romans, tracked the lashes that were delivered to make sure the floggers were accurate with the 40 minus 1 rule.

Brutus raised his whip and so did his partner. Barabbas' eyes bulged as Brutus lashed with a circular motion in super speed. So began the interchange between the floggers; one hit after another whistling in rapid circular motions. The counter caster fumbled the beads in his abacus, nervously counting as fast as he can before screaming out halt, halt! Barabbas received his thirty-nine lashes in less than twenty seconds.

Before the prisoner was dragged away, Brutus looked down at Barabbas and said, "You got off too easy." He then rubbed sand into his victim's wounds ruthlessly. Barabbas arched his back, twitched and hollered in pain. Then Brutus kicked him on the side with the heel of his boot, laughing and wisecracking to entertain the crowd. He then commanded to bring Yeshua to the forum.

(Discretion is advised with regards to the descriptive passages which are necessary. Yeshua gave His life with obedience and understanding to help all people of the

Brutus hanged his custom whip on his personal hook and took a break while waiting for the Roman guard. He saw him walking with Yeshua, got his wooden staff, and headed towards them. Gripping the staff tightly, he pulled it back and struck the back legs of Yeshua, causing Him to bend His knees and plummet to the ground.

To incite the crowd more, Brutus tied a chord around the ankles of Yeshua and proceeded to drag Him on His back towards the front corner pillar. "Untie Him!" the ruffian bellowed as the guards helped Yeshua to His feet, his body shaking in anticipation of what was to come.

Brutus grabbed Yeshua violently by His right shoulder and shuffled Him to the crowd, screaming in an angry voice, "Do any of you want to take His place?" The crowd cowered and backed up slightly. Yeshua slumped still and weak, donning an old king's mantle over His tunic. King Herod had given it to Him as a form of mockery, insinuating He was the "King of the Jews."

Brutus roared to the crowd, "Well, anyone? Not even for a King? Come now!" The flogger spun Yeshua around and pounded his fist into Yeshua's cheekbone, dropping Him to His knees. Yeshua extended His arm to the small knee wall to support Himself, trying to recover and gasping for breath.

The crowd moved when Brutus took one step towards Yeshua and grabbed His hair. He immediately yanked it back, so His face was pointed in the direction of the mob. While holding Yeshua's head up, the ruffian faked a lunge at a lady in front holding a small basket of fruit.

"You would be marvelous to switch positions with Him," Brutus announced in a seductive voice. The lady backed up slowly. The executioner said sweetly, "Come on," then screamed out, "Get over here!" The lady dropped her basket in fright, spun away and ran. Brutus laughed as she scampered away.

"Here!" Brutus barked as he tossed Yeshua towards his partners. One of them had previously flogged Barabbas but the other was fully rested. The ready-to-go flogger was eager to show off his skills.

As Brutus walked over to the short wall to sit, a lictor approached the other executioners and quietly told them to hurry up in no uncertain terms. A lictor was a Roman official entrusted to administer the laws on-site. Brutus released a "Hmp" when he overheard the request, turned his head towards the increasingly rambunctious crowd, and sarcastically said, "We'll see about that, ha!"

The other ruffians tore off the king's mantle from around Yeshua's shoulders and flung it to the onlookers. It heightened the audience's excitement as they viciously tugged and fought for the mantle, tearing it into pieces like hyenas ripping apart their "prey." Yeshua was left with just His subligaculum, an undergarment known as a loincloth.

After the stripping of His garments, Yeshua was forced down to His knees. He was thrown to the ground face down and the new flogger pressed his boot onto His back. Yeshua showed no resistance, stoic in His demeanor. His flogger posed for the audience, as if dominating a hunted kill.

The other executioners tied Yeshua's wrists with slip knots. The more weight a victim had, the more pressure it added to the rope, causing a tighter grip which constricted blood flow to the hands. It happened when the victim can no longer stand and was unable to withstand the pain.

One of the floggers gripped the rope and tugged at it from the center of the pillar between the two rings, trying to hoist Yeshua into position. Brutus yelled, "Put your back into it boy!" Yeshua's limp body lifted off the floor and was positioned into place with His hands above the rings. The ruffian fastened the rope to make it locked and taut.

Yeshua was now hoisted up, famished and weak. He knew that Gabriel's numbing agent would be somewhat ineffective. Watching overhead, Elijah and colleagues were stressed as they watched the flogger checked on the knots on Yeshua's wrists and appeared ready to inflict pain on Yeshua.

Brutus stated to the other flogger, "Ok, it's just us." The two men gathered their own whips, but they will not operate as a team. They would administer the lashes as individuals. Brutus let his partner go first while he walked in the direction of the counter caster. He blocked the counter's view to make it impossible for the counter to do his job.

Alarmed by what was taking place, Elijah and his crew focused a particle spurt beam that targeted the tips of the whip in between hits. The particle beam loosened and severed the barbs attached to two of the four thongs, so the ruffian won't detect the difference in weight. The flogger had already gone over the 40 minus 1 lashing law, leaving the lictor with no choice but to tell Brutus to let the caster counter see.

Brutus replied, "No problem here, let's continue." He looked down at the abacus and declared, "Well it looks like there are only thirteen counted. Twenty-six more to go!" He unleashed twenty-six additional strikes after relieving his partner.

The flagellation marathon left Yeshua in a state of hypovolemic shock, owing to the considerable loss of blood. The metal barbs and sheep bones tore into the subcutaneous tissues, causing excessive skin lacerations. The heavier metal weighted balls on the tips of the whips caused deep contusions with immense pain.

 There was no noise or movement coming from Yeshua. Only quivers from His body as Brutus inflicted lashes and lacerations to parts that were not yet ribbons of bleeding flesh. Yeshua slumped there, passive and obedient the whole time, in and out of consciousness. The crowd was becoming increasingly disturbed and Brutus heard varied cries to stop.

"Enough," the lictor said. "Halt!" Brutus turned to the lictor and proclaimed he had more lashes to give. The cilia of Yeshua's lung had visibly erupted from the torso and was exposed to the air, barely inflating. The lictor decided to use a Roman bylaw which he knew Brutus was well aware of. The law stated that if in the course of flogging a prisoner an internal organ became exposed, the flogging would cease immediately with no exception.

Yeshua was untied from the pillar, then doused with water and cleaned. Later, the slaves attempted to feed Him small pieces of bread and water, but they were unsuccessful. He was then wrapped in a garment which stuck to his wounds like a gauze. Barely able to walk, He was slowly led away from the place of barbarism.

"Wait!" An intoxicated ruffian stumbled while holding a piece from a jujube tree that was woven into a circle with long spider-like thorns. He placed the "crown" atop Yeshua's head, proclaiming, "Look, the King of the Jews!" The ruthless act pierced Yeshua's scalp in numerous areas while the mockery and ridicules persisted.

Pilate was still frantic about the innocence of Yeshua, complaining to his wife and pacing back and forth in the balcony of his palace. He suddenly spotted Barabbas and Yeshua escorted by Roman soldiers and with a crowd of people. He was disturbed and angry when he saw Yeshua being transported by a one-wheeled cart because He was unable to walk.

Pilate turned to his wife and said, "Those barbarians went too far again, but this time on an innocent man!" Shaking his head with disgust, he ordered, "The lavab, lavab!" His assistant quickly fetched the wash basin filled with water as the Roman governor had an idea.

Pilate further explained to the servant, "I want you to follow me to the platform in the courtyard." He was well aware of his responsibilities to the many people waiting for him in the courtyard. He traveled southeast to the back of the palace and entered the part of the complex where the crowd was waiting. The prisoners were brought up to the high platform overlooking the crowd.

Pilate planned to choose Barabbas to be the one executed because he did not want the Nazarene to be put to death. He was hoping the people would choose to release Yeshua, knowing that Barabbas has the worst offenses from all the prisoners held for crucifixion. Barabbas was a murderer, an insurrectionist, a seditionist and most of all, a traitor.

Pilate announced to the charged-up crowd that they would choose who among the prisoners would be set free as part of the Passover tradition. The Roman soldiers shoved Barabbas into view, and the crowd reacted with grunts. The governor looked over to where Yeshua was standing on the opposite right side of the stage and waved his hand aggressively at Him. "Come, come!" he shouted while waving his hand. Yeshua looked confused so Pilate decided to walk over to Him.

As Pilate got closer, he noticed that Yeshua was wearing a crown of thorns and a crimson-stained robe while holding what appeared to be a branch representing a king's scepter. "Ridiculous," he breathed with contempt while seizing the branch out of Yeshua's hand and tossing it to the side. He then brought Yeshua out into the crowd's view so they can see both prisoners clearly.

Pilate waved his left hand to his assistant, indicating he wanted the wash basin brought to him at this instant. He bellowed, "Quiet!" and raised his right hand to simmer the crowd down. He began to wash his hands in front of the crowd while his servant steadily and obediently held the basin.

Pilate proclaimed loudly, "I am innocent of this Man's blood. This is your matter and I wash my hands of this!" Turning to the crowd and drying his hands with a cloth, he pointed to Yeshua and loudly asked the assembled crowd, "Who are you releasing?"

Before Pilate could finish his question, a series of chants erupted abruptly. "Barabbas! Barabbas!" the crowd shouted. The Roman governor moved towards Barabbas asking the crowd, "Barabbas who is guilty of murder and treason?" The crowd further howled Barabbas' name.

Pilate did not know that earlier in the day, the high priest and the Sanhedrin had bribed the Roman guards to stack the crowd against Yeshua. The guards did not let those who sympathized with Yeshua enter the courtyard. Each time Pilate placed his hand above Yeshua's head the crowd screamed, "Crucify Him or we will tell Rome." After a few attempts to sway the crowd, the governor gave up because of the violent screams emanating from what had now become a mob. Yeshua was immediately turned over to be crucified.

Yeshua was brought to the southeast part of the complex, adjacent to Pilate's palace. He waited with two thieves for their final journey to commence. Three Roman horsemen untied individually a beam of wood that was attached to the rear of their horses' saddle skirt. They would be the cross beams for each of the doomed, to be carried up to the Mount of Golgotha.

Two emotionless soldiers placed and positioned the timber on Yeshua's shoulders. He let out a short cry as the rough wood pressed against His existing wounds. It was now settled against His neck, shoulders and back. Every movement delivered immediate pain and He hesitated to move forward. He peered up the long winding road ahead.

One of the soldiers on a horse said, "Pilate had given orders for this to be mounted above His head on the cross." He tossed a sign to his colleague who looped a cord through it and hanged it like a necklace around Yeshua's neck. It moved back and forth Yeshua's chest wounds as the soldier chuckled at what it said, "Yeshua of Nazareth, King of the Jews."

The action of hanging that sign was the third happening out of the norm. The first unusual occurrence was Yeshua being presented a king's cloak and scepter. The second was receiving a crown of thorns. The theoretical antithesis of all three incidents correlated with the veil from His Mother [sign], the nimbus halo [thorns] and the patina [cloak & scepter].

The winding route began from a distance of about half a mile and was called the Via Dolorosa, the "way of sorrows." This road winded between structures, and then headed towards open land at the fork juncture. A division of Roman legionnaires lined up along the path leading up to Golgotha, some on horseback and many on foot to herd the people away and provide a clear pathway. Their orders are explicit: keep the prisoners alive until crucified.

Stones started flying towards the captives, coinciding with sadistic laughter, and Yeshua fell onto one knee due to the weight of the hundred-pound beam. A mounted soldier snapped his long whip, whirling and encircling its ends at the corner of Yeshua's burden. He hoisted the timber with a strong tug, balancing Yeshua's load and assisting Him back to His feet.

The day had reached its hottest temperature as Yeshua navigated the curved dusty pathways. He struggled as he perspired what little water was left in His body. There were people who attempted to help Him, bringing cool cloths to relieve His heated pain, but only women were allowed to pass as they were not a threat to hinder the journey.

Certain Faction members had been approved and allowed by the Temporal Watchmen to witnesses Yeshua's final day. Elijah and his colleagues were distraught, trying hard to separate their emotions and maintain sobriety. The prophet moved a cloud to block the sun's harsh rays beating upon Yeshua.

Yeshua lifted His head to see how much more was the distance to Golgotha, which is Hebrew for "Place of Skulls." His ears were hearing muffled noises. His eyes were fogged, His breath was shallow, and His head was limp. He lost His balance again and stumbled forward, the wooden beam landing hard onto the sandy ground. Consequently, He fell and landed on His back.

For fear that Yeshua might die before crucifixion, one of the Roman soldiers looked for a man to assist Him with the remaining trek. The mounted officer pointed to a bystander who was standing next to cart loaded with bushels of crops.

"Help this Man, instead of watching Him!"

The farmer said, "Don't you see I have others with me?"

The soldier put his hand on his sword and drew it. The man gave muddled instructions to his companions where they would meet up later and went to Yeshua. Looking over from the corner of His eye, Yeshua wondered where this man came from who was supporting His every step.

The crowd thinned at a leveled and narrow passage and it was there where Yeshua caught sight of Mary. She hesitated in shock, her breath stolen from her, before she gathered herself and dashed towards her Son. "My Son, My Son!" she exclaimed as she moved near Him. The guard, having compassion, let the meeting take place. Her hands were shaking as she tried to touch Him, not knowing where to feel Him in fear of causing additional pain. She touched His palm with her fingertips, feeling the contours of each of His fingers and realizing this will be the last time she will touch her beloved Son.

Yeshua gave His mother a compassionate look of sorrow and when Mary tried to kiss Him, she saw the crown and withdrew. Any contact on His bruised face and cut dried lips would result in further pain. She started bawling and convulsing, and was about to faint. As the disciple John caught her from behind, Yeshua realized that His wounds and sufferings had pierced His mother's heart, crushing her.

Yeshua addressed Mary in a gentle tone, "Dear mother, your heart is so troubled. Stay close to Me yet have the virtue of patience and fortitude, for this is Thy Father's will."

The Roman soldier commanded Yeshua to proceed. He dragged Himself forward as the distance widened between Him and His mother. Mary extended her arms, hands wide open, as she dreamt about her spirit being with her Son's spirit. John held her shoulder to support her.

As Yeshua veered left and dropped out of sight, Mary fell on her knees with cries of sorrow and pain. John assisted her back to Her feet while the crowd relentlessly tormented her Son. She attempted to collect herself while she listened to the elevated volume of ridicule and mockery. It embittered her so much she turned to the disciple and said, "Take me to the top!"

CHAPTER SEVENTEEN

CRUCIFIXION

Elijah, hovering silently in the clouds, was observing vigilantly and steadily and was ready for a multitude of outcomes. His was the only vessel allowed in such close proximity while the other follower-ships were watching high in the ionosphere and magnetosphere. Never did a coordinated union of species from different worlds and times shared in one moment like the one they were about to witness.

Yeshua finally reached the summit and lifted His head up to see three stipes (stakes) of gray weathered wood protruding from the plateau at the top of Golgotha. Each of the stipes was equal in height of seven plus feet and looked ready to anticipate anguish of mind and body.

Yeshua was thoroughly exhausted as He was no longer receiving any assistance. He waited barely able to stand. He had a blurred view of His soon to be cross, knowing that the middle stipe was His and His alone. It was somewhat more forward than the other two stakes.

Yeshua gathered his strength to lift His head and look at the cloud where Elijah was watching. He bowed to the cloud to indicate He can see this through. Elijah was emotionally exhausted, and his heart was wrenched with grief.

There was an invisible but understood boundary for the spectators in the crucifixion area. The area behind the stipes was designated for Roman guards only. They sat tall on their horses with an occasional shouting of orders, usually coming from the high-ranking officers.

There was an eerie silence as the people watched Yeshua obediently awaiting His crucifixion. The Lamb had been led to the slaughter. He stood there wearing a heavy lavender and tan tinged garment, stuck to a plank of wood with ropes railed to His arms. His head was down with only the surface of His hair visible, a crown of thorns nested onto His scalp.

The crowd became apprehensive as they witnessed the execution of an innocent Man they helped condemn. Two soldiers marched over and started grappling with the timber on Yeshua's shoulders, one on each side. They counted in unison to three, then lifted the heavy wood and dragged Yeshua.

The two soldiers spun Yeshua clockwise who staggered while turning and standing. The Romans were having fun with this cruel scene. They continually tossed and spun Yeshua while they stripped off His clothes except for the undergarment. The soldiers took and divided his clothes by casting lots, confirming a prophecy that appeared in scripture.

Elijah watched the soldiers snickered with laughter like a pack of hyenas. One of the ruffians waited patiently as he shuffled three iron nails in his left hand, creating an annoying clanging sound. He had a heavy hammer dangling from his right arm.

Yeshua fell to His knees and was tossed back. His knees bent as He collapsed backwards to the wood and the ground. The force was so great that it sent a cry into the sky. The jugular vein on His neck pulsated with pain while His eyes were almost completely shut, with only a sliver of an opening.

Then suddenly, His eyes fired wide open and His back convulsed upward as the first of the three nails of pierced His left wrist. The nail spiked its way to the timber, grabbing entry into the surface of the wood and severing the median nerve but "without fracturing a single bone" (also prophesied in the scriptures). The nail's pathway was guided by a frequency marked and steered by one of Elijah's crew.

The ruffian took the next nail and spun it in his hand. He pointed the tip of the nail on Yeshua's right wrist then came down hard with the hammer. There was a cracking noise and sparks because it was an indirect hit. Four more swings were needed. They pushed the wrist extra tight to the wood, causing needles of numbness in His hand and unbearable pain to His wrist.

The soldier doing the hammering lifted up his head, got up from his kneeling position and spewed out a command, "Proceed!" Taking the rope, he tossed it over the top of the highest point of the stipe. Another soldier received the rope from the opposite side, making sure the rope was resting at the highest point of the stipe.

The rope was now on top of the stipe, taut and ready to be pulled. But the Roman soldier told his partner, "No! I'll take care of it!" He wanted to work solo to show off his strength. Grabbing and tangling the rope around his wrist, the soldier dug his feet into the ground and pulled the rope using his body weight. The beam lifted off the ground and hoisted Yeshua, his back hitting against the stipe.

Torment and laughter erupted from the crowd, amused at what they were seeing. Yeshua's feet left the surface of the Earth for the final time, hoisted in short interval tugs. His body ascended to the destined point. The front of the stipe was smooth from previous crucifixions of the many condemned who were dragged up its stem.

A soldier stood on a wooden ladder to guide and hold the body until the cross-wood beam was put in place. The onlookers ranted and joked about the soldier's height who shook his head and went about his work. From around Yeshua's neck, he removed the sign that Pilate had instructed to hang above the cross and looped it around the protruding beam. After climbing down from the ladder, he held it and flung it towards where he believed the teasing came from. The crowd stepped backward as the soldier snarled with satisfaction.

The ruffian with the heavy hammer came back with the remaining nail, the largest one to be used. He began to wrap over Yeshua's right leg across the top of His left leg with enormous pressure. Legs locked, Yeshua was nailed at the right tarsi (area of bones) with the long spike. Again, no bones were broken as Yeshua began the final stages of His crucifixion. Crucifixion began in Persia, but the Romans perfected it as a form of torturous capital punishment that by design resulted in a slow death with maximum pain.

Elijah turned off the audio. There were monitors showing the three crosses on top of the mount, the vital signs of all three victims, and every individual in attendance, including horses and dogs up to three furlongs away. Elijah remained silent with his comrades and watched from an aerial viewpoint, able to see and analyze anything and everything, no matter how small or what angle.

Yeshua reflected and held dearly to the memories of His life, covered in dried blood and hardened dirt. Now that all the prisoners were nailed to their crosses, most of the entertainment was finished. The work of the soldiers was done and most of them took their belongings and vanished into the crowd. The waiting began with some guards left behind to finish the job.

There were discussions amongst Elijah's crew, and they paid attention to the disciple John taking Mother Mary towards the crosses. The restrictions had been lifted by the Roman soldiers to allow permissible distance near the crosses. Mary stopped in front of her Son's cross and dropped on Her knees, unable to take a step closer. Elijah, observing from above, could only see her deep blue mantle cascading on both sides of her weeping body.

The sun's position changed such that Elijah's cloud was no longer blocking it. The warm rays bathed Yeshua and Mary, and together They took in the same light. Their spirits communed with God, pure and without regret.

As His last moments were upon Him, Yeshua couldn't move His nape because of the crown of thorns inhibiting Him from putting his head back. His neck stayed bent over as a priest stood and stared at Him with a puzzled look. Nicademous, who was one of the priests who questioned Jesus from the very beginning and had doubts, began to admire Him in a factual light. The priest felt an innocent Man was dying on the cross.

Nicademous' thoughts slowly came together, and he had an epiphany. He began to recite the scripture aloud, particularly the prophet Isaiah's words as he stared directly at Yeshua hanging from the cross. "He was pierced through for our transgressions, He was crushed for our iniquities, and by His scourging we are healed. All of us are like sheep and have gone astray, He is and will be," the priest breathed out as tears rolled from his eyes.

As Yeshua neared death, the clouds accumulated, and the darkness increased. The sky turned a dark grey ash as the ominous clouds carried out the Articles of Faith's doctrine. In spite of the bad weather, only a few of the onlookers left as they were curious as to what would happen next.

Elijah paid full attention to the main display which was the visual and audio monitor. It was the complete tracker of the energy within Yeshua's nimbus. Once His physical body expired, what followed was the halo dimming process of the nimbus all the way to a subatomic level.

Suddenly, the sound alerts went off when the crew heard, "Father forgive them, they know not what they do, give them but that one day." Yeshua exhaled weakly and looked down at His mother and John. He introduced them as the family He was leaving behind before letting out a death rattle as He feverishly tried to breathe.

Elijah's stomach was knotted tight, trying to withstand what was happening. He bowed his head, seeing that the end is near. He tried to stay strong and be alert, but his tears overflowed regardless of his attempt to control them. He reached out his hand at the image of Yeshua while his other hand was cupped over his mouth.

Yeshua spoke again, "My God! My God! Have I forsaken You? Beholding to Thyself!" He lifted His head as high as it could go but the wooden barbs from His crown of thorns stopped Him. Both His arms and legs were limp and without movement. His jugular vein throbbed with great effort as His heart pumped harder to push blood through His body.

Yeshua knew His breaths were numbered, lifeless in-fact except for the contractions of some involuntary muscles in His body. Unexpectedly, a ventral convulsion began in His chest, startling those who had remained. He called out, "Eli! Eli!" (As quoted from the

Articles of Faith, "He had to die with absolute abandonment from the heavens; time will heal as time returns.")

Elijah sadly nodded, his swollen eyes full to the brim with tears. He sent a pulse of amplified electromagnetic field-waves into the dark black clouds hovering above the entire area. Lightning struck, followed by thunderous blasts that shook the ground. It was the confirmation response of Elijah, acknowledging Yeshua's statement. Yeshua nodded once as His head dipped forward.

His excessive injuries were causing Yeshua a severe loss of blood and essential fluids. His chief arteries struggled to push the flow of blood and His air-pockets were slowly being replaced with liquids. There were very little spaces left to take in the last few breaths, each one becoming shorter and shorter, and asphyxia was inevitable. "I thirst" He uttered with little movement from His mouth.

Surprised at Yeshua's request, a soldier soaked a sponge with wine mixed with gall/myrrh, placed it at the tip of a hyssop plant stem about three feet in length, and brought the liquid up to His lips. Yeshua refused to drink it, glanced at the heavens one last time, and exhaled with a final convulsion, "It is finished, Father, into Thy hands I commend My spirit."

Silent Reflections

After His final words, Yeshua's beautiful blue eyes disappeared into His heavily laden eyelids to mark consummation. His head flaccidly yielded to a forward position where it remained. There was silence all around. Three soldiers at the base of the cross did something unprecedented, taking to one knee. They were not affected by the explosions of thunder as they removed their helmets, bowed their heads, and paid their respects to what they knew was a divine moment.

The three o'clock hour struck, timing Yeshua's death with the exact moment the Passover lambs' throats were slit to signify the sacrificial offering. During Yeshua's childhood, John the Baptist used that phrase and referred to Him as the Lamb of God who ushered in this moment (Lamb of God who takes away the sins of the world).

While the Jewish priests in the city collected a lamb's blood in bowls for their ceremonious ritual, Elijah unleashed a thunderous rain from the large dark ash cloud following the directives in the Articles of Faith. Yeshua's body was lowered from the cross with great difficulty because of the lightning and pouring rain.

It was routine practice to break the legs of the victim to ensure they were dead but in Yeshua's case, He already was. To double-check, one of the soldiers took a long sharp lance and pierced it upward between the ribs on His right side. The tip of the spear penetrated seven inches to the targeted point, releasing pleural and pericardial fluid along with little blood. It was done for two reasons; first to make sure that the person was dead and secondly to have an easier time handling the corpse. The release of fluids would make the corpse lighter and prevent additional swelling or expansion.

When Yeshua was fully removed from the cross, one of the soldiers gently laid Him in Mary's arms. Mary moved under her Son to capture His limp body, rocking Him like a child. His left arm dangled lifelessly as the back of His hand brushed against the mud repeatedly. Mary cradled her Son close to her heart, her tears joining the rain as they fell and splattered to the ground. The heartbreaking moment was reminiscent of Mary holding her Newborn in the manger with Joseph, whispering to Yeshua a song of King Solomon.

Elijah and his colleagues sent amplified signals from the heavens, concentrating a magnetic wave at the rear of Golgotha where all the crucified bodies were thrown into a large pit and covered. Along with the deluge of rain and thunder, an earthquake rattled the whole mountain. Many in Jerusalem witnessed the weather anomalies and watched as Calvary received the wrath of the gods.

The mountainous ground spewed open, pushing up thousands of dead bodies out of the land. The bodies began to hurl and tumble down the mountainside. The people ran away in fear, unable to tell the difference between the tumbling corpses and the fleeing spectators.

John, the apostle, comforted Mary, saying, "Do not worry; the mountain will be calm soon." Almost immediately after reassuring her, the clouds started to dissipate, and the ground became still.

John politely told Mary about two Jewish priests who wanted to help take Yeshua's body away from this place and give Him a proper burial. They would like to donate a newly prepared tomb. John said softly, "Their names are Joseph of Arimathea, the owner of the plot, and Nicodemus, a priest convinced that Yeshua is the Messiah."

Joseph of Arimathea addressed his request to Pilate, asking for possession of Yeshua's body and taking the initiative to purchase new linens for His burial. Pilate agreed because of the honorable reputation that preceded Joseph. With tears in her eyes, Mary nodded to say yes as John helped her to her feet.

Tomb

Joseph and Nicodemus carefully wrapped the body in fine linens in accordance with Jewish tradition. The women who followed Yeshua applied the myrrh and fragrantly sweet oils they had brought. Quickly, they gathered the body as sunset was upon them and the Sabbath was at hand. The tomb was near Joseph's property, a short distance from his house.

Yeshua's burial place was hewed from an already existing rock formation. The enormous, rounded rock used for the door seal was the most difficult part of the construction. According to Joseph of Arimathea, it took the same time to mine the whole tomb and to make the door. Inside, there was a natural bench formation for the body's final resting place.

Joseph and Nicodemus were wealthy and well-noted affiliates of the Sanhedrin but were becoming disciples of Yeshua. Joseph, who was waiting for the coming of the kingdom his whole life, saw it in Yeshua of Nazareth. It fell in line with the Articles of Faith that foretold not only a new garden tomb, but one that befitted royalty.

Chapter Eighteen

The Resurrection

Yeshua's body lay within the linen, in the tomb, without light. Beneath the supple sheet, His legs lay straight and parallel while His arms crossed and overlapped on top of His lower abdomen. His right hand was laid gently on top of the wound on His left wrist.

The Jewish High Priest and the Sanhedrin opposing Yeshua felt that He might be more dangerous to them dead, than when He was alive. They asked Pontius Pilate to secure guards at their expense and protect the seal on the tomb. The priests informed Pilate that they heard rumors that the disciples might stage a possible rising from the dead ritual. Pilate reluctantly gave them what they wanted while complaining in a disrespectful manner.

Recapturing his disposition, Elijah waited patiently as he stared at the holographic display showing the moments since Yeshua's demise. He continuously searched for certain performance parameters using a bio-energy medical monitor and waited for the miraculous chemical reaction to occur signaling the regeneration process.

The crew continued to transmit data from a biotelemetry main monitoring station locked on and focused directly inside the tomb. They made minor adjustments and tracked the nucleic acids of Yeshua's body tissues, organelles, cell receptors, enzymes, and antibodies which were all linked to the patina's re-birth.

Suddenly, a ping alert light came on and Elijah alerted his colleagues with joyous emotions. He switched to the main monitor and observed the subatomic particles quivering as heat and motion were detected. Excitement filled the room as they waited for the thirty-three hours to complete the patina process.

The Roman guards stood rigid in front and above the tomb which was outer sealed with mortar cement. They were stalwart and confident in their stance, unknowing of the phenomenon that was taking place inside the tomb.

Elijah monitored the activity within the tomb and saw orangey yellow lights spewing from all sides of the shroud that encompassed Yeshua's entire corpse, glowing outward in a blaze of glory. The radiation scorched the shroud that covered Yeshua, leaving an imprint of His Being on the cloth that draped His body. (This cloth is now known as the Shroud of Turin.)

As the first hours of that Sunday approached, the angel Gabriel descended from the sky and hovered right above the tomb. Blinding lights emanated from his back and shook the grounds beneath to break the seal around the stone door. The Roman guards, in disoriented panic, would later describe a man with bird type wings moving, flying, and descending.

All the Roman guards ran from their posts in a frenzy to tell Pilate what they just witnessed. With the area deserted, Gabriel and James the Apostle linked the center of gravity to the stone covering the entrance to the tomb. The two easily floated the elliptical stone thirty meters away from the entrance of the cave and laid it gently on its side where it was originally quarried from.

Elijah sent Gabriel and James into the tomb with a tunic made from a filament resembling fine silk, with gold braids bordering the neckline as well as the sleeves. Yeshua's sandals and leather woven strap belt that Elijah gifted to Him years back were also placed alongside Him. Afterwards, both men left the tomb and stood at attention in the garden.

Suddenly, there was movement within the tomb and a shimmering light appeared at the opening. A gleaming and luminous figure came into view and revealed to the universe the Risen Christ, the promised Messiah. Yeshua sparkled as He looked up to the heavens. Elijah's trumpet sounds could be heard from miles away to signify a new era has begun.

Yeshua turned to Gabriel and James with arms wide open and smiled, giving thanks for all they have done. He then ascended upward to greet an excited Elijah, who was glowing with happiness as he received Him. All of the pain and fear from the past days were gone, and they were ready to continue the mission of the Articles of Faith.

The Articles of Faith had Yeshua appearing at certain geographical points at precise times to fulfill His vocation. It was stated in the Articles of Faith that it was extremely important that women be the first to see the risen Christ. It would carry a symbolic meaning throughout the ages, showing importance and respect for the female species. The action also increased the number of people that can be saved.

Salome, also called Mary, was (one of the three Mary's) the mother of the apostles James and John and interacted with Elijah during his life. She was like an aunt to him because of the close relationship of his father, Aligious, with Salome's husband, Zebedee. Salome was told to search out the other two Mary's, Mary the Mother and Mary Magdalene, thus gathering them for the good news.

As the women entered the tomb, they found the shroud neatly folded into three angles.

Yeshua made five profound appearances, one of which was of a personal nature. He visited His mother before doing anything else. He was worried her heart would fail due to the trauma she went through. He visited other key people and places the following days with His ability to levitate and bi-locate. He worked closely with Elijah, his colleagues, and the apostles Peter, James, and John for the final section of the Articles of Faith.

They were setting their sights on the Second Coming. Yeshua gave the remaining disciples their final instructions and the geographical regions they will be sent to for evangelization. Yeshua's departure for the Second Coming took place exactly 40 days after His Resurrection and was called the "Ascension."

In accordance with God's will, Yeshua's ascent into the heavens was punctuated with angelic psalms. Elijah greeted Him with excitement and had a short private conversation with Him about His last few days. They immediately focused onto tomorrow, leaving this time period and traveling two millennia forward.

Chapter Nineteen

The Second Coming

According to the Planetary Union Guidelines, when the human species reached technological advancements that can affect the space time continuum, the implementation of the Faction Integration Program (FIP) would commence. The (unstable) volatility among the varied human species made them a potential threat to the Factions (Planetary Union).

The future engagement between the Factions and humankind was dependent upon the Hadron Collider in Switzerland reaching the capability to create temporal porthole entries (space/time capabilities). This pinnacle point of advanced human technology had been long awaited with Yeshua and other great prophets gifting their wisdom throughout the millennia.

Originally, only approximately one hundred forty-four thousand people would be redeemed to move the planet forward before the existence of Yeshua. Because of Him, over half a million people would be chosen instead. In addition, His works benefitted billions of others that have passed on through the millennia.

The reason that 6.6 billion people were not chosen for this chapter in human history was because they did not meet the criterion set by the governing council. Even though the Factions had the ability to activate the dormant DNA strands that would enable all humankind to use their brain's full ability towards a new consciousness and amplified intelligence, it was reserved exclusively for the chosen humans.

Elijah, Peter, James, and John were given the privilege and honor to be the forerunner to Yeshua's Second Coming. It would be omnipresent in multi-locations throughout the Earth with Yeshua represented by His bio-frequency signature. One's personal bio-signature would be compared and passed through Yeshua's to determine if the person met the important criterion. To be selected, the bio-signature must not fall below 66.6% to His spiritual imprinted signature.

The selected few would be raptured and transfigured. There's a forty-day preparatory expedition to introduce the history and present the current existence of the twelve Factions. Those who chose to finish this forty-day passage should be committed to the end.

Anyone who could not complete this forty-day journey had the option to return to Earth and join the remaining 6.6 billion. Upon hearing this, a few of the chosen ones elected to return to Earth because they had left family behind. They were able to live out the rest of their lives as they deemed fit in accordance with Elijah's request to the Council for "mercy" rather than extinction or Armageddon.

For those who finished the journey, it marked a new dawn on Earth with peace and harmony for all.

Ascension

The third day arrived and Yeshua appeared strategically throughout the Earth, hovering or standing above squares, streets, and churches. He looked angelic with waves of transparent reflections coming from His being, and lines of bright whites when He moved.

Delivered in all languages specific to each person, Yeshua spoke, "Do not feel deluded by the peace and prosperity of choices. Surely, we have needfulness for a divine purpose. You have the dynamic capacity to choose where to go and what to do. Do not limit yourself by taking the easy road in life. I speak of transcending beyond this life for your earthly existence is simply one flap of a sparrow's wing."

There were people who heard Yeshua and came towards Him while to others, His message fell on deaf ears. Assemblies of prophets from different religious periods conveyed and delivered other messages. The most profound message was, "You can live in a world filled with peace, with no diseases and endless possibilities for thousands of years to come! Still, many are despondent, wanting to live their life without veering."

The World that understood the messages was captivated by Yeshua's profound words of dedication to the acceptance of who they could be. His radiance filled all of the Earth, the people gazing intently with eagerness and serious attention. Then He dematerialized.

CHAPTER TWENTY

INTEGRATION

In the "Temporal Exodus" of the chosen, more than a century would pass before the integration began. The Factions helped in the collaborative effort called the Zion Elysium Project (ZEP).

ZEP was a vast undertaking of rebuilding the Earth with eco-friendly materials and masonry that would stand the test of time. A glorious, picturesque environment was built using sacred geometry on a natural energy grid.

The presence of technology in the ZEP agenda increased the capacity to forge a heightened awareness for all. Inserted were certain technologies such as the internet, mobile devices, microwave apparatuses, and other technical upgrades.

The biggest part of the ZEP program was the Black Opt Culvert Operation designed to make mankind responsible for their own future. Governments of leading countries funneled an enormous amount of money and resources into the project for human survival and preservation. The political parties in charge created a capitalistic growth platform for accumulation of economic wealth, while another political group absorbed the wealth and funneled it into the operation, creating a facade of helping everyone.

Supervised and assisted by many of the Factions, the initiative should be up and running by the 2030's. Judgment Day would see the (new) human Faction joining the Union of Planets.

The options for the chosen few (500,000+) would be to return to Earth in the future in a "New Order of the Ages," or take residence in an off-planet facility to learn the Faction's symmetry and explore its projects throughout the sector.

Elijah and Jesus rested, assured of what the future holds and not worried of what could have been. They had overcome the impossible, helping and saving not only the chosen few but the entire future population from the Apocalypse.

Elijah's total embrace of his father's vision was a compliment and tribute to his mastery and remarkable talent personified by Love and Devotion. "Blessed are those who embrace these new challenges."

THE BOOK OF ELIJAH

****

This tome is the second aliquot part of "The Integration" which is the next volume to be written. Once again, keep in mind that these writings are not here to sway your beliefs but to take from them as you would like. Take the positive traits from what you encountered.

Postscript:

The Resurrection Story appears in more than five locations in the Bible. In several episodes in the Four Gospels, Jesus foretold His coming death and resurrection, which He stated was the plan of God the Father (Articles of Faith). Christians view the Resurrection of Jesus as part of a plan for salvation and redemption by atoning for man's sin (DNA). Belief in a bodily resurrection of the dead was well established within some segments of Jewish society in the centuries leading up to the time of Christ, as recorded by Daniel 12:2 from the mid-2nd century B.C.

Messiah and Savior: There are many associations attached to Elijah and Jesus, what and how they are represented, yet the results of their actions and contributions seemingly supersede the distinctive part.

Author recommends the extended version of this book on Audio.

(Amazon Audible) Title: Elijah, The Secret Prospective.

By Robert Rasch

****

Mystical Note: Once again, this volume is a timed release for April 5th, 2017 to coincide with the historical Resurrection of Jesus which was also on April 5th. This coincidence of dates is not by accident. According to Elijah's Flexion Team, it is

currently 20 years from this date, on April 5th, 2037, that there will be the New Dawn of the Ages, "The Second Coming."

ABOUT THE AUTHOR

Robert Rasch is the author of Elijah, a traditional story with a modern twist. His writing provides a new perspective on the origin of humanity, with his unique approach to telling a story that has been told many times. His ability to mix "coincidental-science" with the Old and New Testaments is intriguing. Other writings Robert Rasch is working on include: Dead Ringer, Victorian Girls, Sleepers 72, Opulence, a romance comedy, and View Finder, science fiction. Screen writes, Ebe and Flash Forward. Capanni27@gmail.com.

www.ingramcontent.com/pod-product-compliance
Lightning Source LLC
Chambersburg PA
CBHW061545050726
47593CB00002B/903